ACHILL ISLAND

by

Valerie Hansard

Grosvenor House
Publishing Limited

This book is published by
Grosvenor House Publishing Ltd
Link House
140 The Broadway, Tolworth, Surrey, KT6 7HT.
www.grosvenorhousepublishing.co.uk

A CIP record for this book
is available from the British Library

ISBN 978-1-83975-692-4

Chapter One

It was Saturday. Liam crept down the uncarpeted staircase and stood outside the front room, also called the parlour, where Dad was working at his desk. On Saturdays Dad could often be persuaded to take him and his brother, Dermot to Achill Island for a swim. Liam stood outside the closed door for a few moments wondering if he should knock. Dad could be a little stroppy if interrupted while working. Sometimes he could even be a bit rough. Inside he heard a faint rustling, then the scraping of a chair. When he heard footsteps coming towards the door he stepped aside as it opened. It wouldn't look good if he were caught spying. Dad went to the bottom of the stairs and called up: 'Liam! The rain's easing off. How about a swim off Keel Strand?'

Liam and Dermot gathered up their swimming gear and piled into the car. In less than half an hour they arrived on Achill Island. Sean O'Malley drove across the narrow causeway, joining what over fifty years ago had once been an island, to the mainland. He parked the car on a solid stony patch at the upper end of the six mile sandy beach. Already wearing their swimsuits, the boys ran into the sea. They were both good swimmers, an essential skill for swimming in the Atlantic Ocean off the

West Coast of Ireland. There were waves, currents and a huge spray.

'Race you into the next wave!' called Liam, as they both dived into the high wave, foaming at the top. As the wave flattened and reached the shoreline, they surfaced, Dermot barely an arms length ahead. Liam turned over on his back and laughed.

'You won. But only just. And you are two years older than me.'

They swam and played around in the sea for another fifteen minutes.

'I've had enough,' said Dermot. 'Let's get out now.'

They negotiated more waves and reached the shore. Walking up on the firm damp sand, they waved to the car in the distance. Seeing his sons approaching, Sean sounded a welcoming hoot on the horn and started the engine to warm up the car, his usual procedure on a cool day. As the boys arrived, Sean opened the rear passenger door.

'Well done, boys. Did you enjoy your swim?'

'It was terrific, Dad,' replied Liam, climbing into the back seat. As they dried off and dressed, Sean drove the car onto the narrow unsurfaced road towards the Achill Island causeway. The swim is a good idea, he thought. The boys don't have much other physical exercise in the long summer holidays. In less than half an hour they were back in Westport. Sean drove down the main street, as usual quiet and deserted on a Saturday afternoon. Turning off, he arrived in a narrow rundown side street, finally stopping outside a small, shabby semi-detached Victorian house. He got out of the car and walked up the uneven path to the front door, badly in need of a coat of paint. The front garden also needed work.

Overgrown shrubs and weeds straggled over the path, obscuring the lower half of the bay window. Gathering up their wet swimming gear, Dermot and Liam followed their father into the house and went upstairs to their bedroom to change their clothes. The house was too small for five growing children, but Sean didn't have sufficient financial resources to buy a larger property. Aged twelve, Liam already resented having to share a bedroom with his fourteen year old brother.

There were three older children. Donal, twenty years old, was out all day working as a farmhand on two local farms. He left home at seven in the morning, returning at seven in the evening. The farm work was extremely arduous, and after a simple meal he went straight to bed. No one in the family commented on his increasingly shabby and aging appearance. No one was able to offer him any advice.

There were two girls: Sinead, aged eighteen and Nora, two years younger, who both worked locally as shop assistants. They couldn't wait to get married and move away from Westport and the constrictions of the O'Malley family, but so far no one had proposed.

But the greatest burden for the entire family was being raised without a mother. Since the death of his wife, Eileen, almost ten years ago Sean was forced to shoulder all the practical and emotional burdens on his own. It was he who made the decisions for the entire family – alone. He knew that when his two daughters reached puberty he would make mistakes: and he did. And his daughters resented it. It was a little easier making decisions for his sons, but mistakes were still made. Sometimes Sean felt he should look around for new adult help: a partner, even a wife. But in such a small remote town as Westport there was very little choice. And above all he couldn't spare the time. So the O'Malley family soldiered on in a house full of dust, grime and cobwebs, flanked by a garden full of weeds and dead flowers.

Before the outbreak of World War II, the West of Ireland was a popular tourist destination. Travellers either flew to Dublin and drove west across the flat boggy terrain of the centre of the country, or they flew directly to Shannon Airport and hired a self-drive car. The most popular route was directly north, through Galway Town, along Lough Corrib and through James Joyce Country. The more intrepid travellers made it to Achill Island to admire the bleak mountain views immortalised by the painter, Paul Henry, who lived there for many years. But no one stopped for long in Westport. It was too bleak and empty. Once war had broken out almost no one travelled anywhere, so Westport became more and more isolated.

Liam was now in his second year at the Christian Brothers' School, the only secondary school in Westport. It was extremely religious and very strict. Making friends with children of the opposite sex was strongly disapproved of, both by local families and the strict teaching of the Catholic Church. At all the schools in the West of Ireland boys and girls were required to sit on opposite sides of the classroom and were strongly discouraged from mixing at playtime. Liam felt constricted, almost imprisoned, constantly wondering how he could escape. Fortunately, he enjoyed his academic work and was top of his class. As it was the only school for miles around, it accommodated boarders as well as day pupils. Sadly, the boarders were at the bottom of the pile. The food was poor and up to ten children slept in dormitories in hard, uncomfortable beds with coarse, scratchy sheets. Rumours of paedophilia constantly abounded and although no particular priests' names were mentioned, suspicion fell on several of the older, more senior teachers. None of the abused pupils were ever questioned or helped. The abuse was a frightening, hidden secret.

It was the visits to Achill Island that began to form Liam's main point of rescue. It was not only the swimming he enjoyed so much; there were also the fishing trips with two of the local fishermen. One sunny morning in late July 1941, he and Dermot were scrambling out of the sea ready to return to their Dad's car, when a small boat pulled up beside them.

'Hello, lads! You're a couple of great swimmers! Fancy a trip?'

'What – now? We'll have to tell Dad. He's waiting to drive us home.'

'No, not now. Later in the day. We fish for mackerel and they don't like the sun, so we go out in the evening. Ever eaten mackerel?'

'I don't know,' replied Liam doubtfully. 'Dad never tells us what the fish is called. He just expects us to eat it.'

The fisherman laughed. 'That's okay. I understand. How would you both like to come out with us tomorrow evening? Let's say six o'clock? You needn't let us know. Just turn up if you can. By the way, I'm Brendan and this is Paddy.'

'I'm Liam and this is my brother, Dermot. Sorry, my hand is wet.'

And so began, for Liam and Dermot, a very special new experience. At first their father objected to driving them to Achill Island 'just for a fishing trip.' But Liam and Dermot enjoyed the fishing so much, that Sean soon came round to the idea.

In 1944, by the time he had turned sixteen, Liam had become increasingly aware of the constraints of life in Westport. Out of school hours there was little to do and nowhere new to go in such a small isolated town. War had now been raging for five years and most young people were kept on a very tight leash. Although Ireland was officially a neutral country, more Irishmen than British per capita of the population actually fought at the front, and the Irish people still expected German bombs to fall at any time. In the early days of the war several had fallen on Dublin, and although no one had been killed, the fear still remained. Social life in Westport was extremely limited. There were pubs, of course, but only open to those over eighteen years of age. There were no cafés or restaurants and one very rundown hotel.

Sometimes Father O'Brien had mooted the idea of Liam going to university. They weren't free, but it was possible he might win a scholarship to University College in Dublin. Trinity College was ranked considerably higher than University College, but Liam knew it was out of the question. It was considered a hell-hole of Protestant apostasy by the then notorious Catholic Archbishop of Dublin, John Charles McQuaid, who had forbidden all Irish Roman Catholics to study there.

Liam discussed his prospects with his Dad. Sean confessed to Liam that he had always wanted to study law at university and become a barrister, but due to lack of money he had been forced to leave school aged fourteen. Working long hours in a greengrocers, he had saved up enough money to take a year's course as a clerk of the court, hoping it would lead him further up the ladder. But over thirty years later he was still a clerk in Galway Town Court.

So Liam kept his head down, worked hard and did so well in his Leaving Certificate that he won a scholarship to University College in Dublin. He was over the moon and couldn't believe his luck. Finally, at the age of eighteen he was about to escape, at least during term time, from the restrictions of his birthplace. True to form, after three more years of intense study, he gained a first class degree. When the result came through, Liam's tutor suggested he should apply for a pupillage as a trainee barrister in London.

'There's a Bar Professional Training Course in Lincoln's Inn Fields,' he explained. 'In the legal profession it's called BPTC. Ever heard of it?'

'No. Never. How much will it cost? You know I have no money.'

'You'll receive a small salary and accommodation. Why don't you fly over to London and have a look round? I'll pay your expenses. You're worth it.'

Liam was so overcome with gratitude that he wanted to hug his tutor. But something stopped him. It might be a mistake. In a few weeks it was all arranged. Liam obtained a pupillage in the prestigious Law Courts in Lincoln's Inn Fields: another very big step up on the Ladder of Life.

In 1949, now aged twenty-one, Liam discovered that life in London was a completely different world to what he had become accustomed to in Dublin. His accommodation consisted of one small room with a kitchen and bathroom shared with two other tenants. It was situated in a Victorian house in St. Baldwin's Gardens, a narrow street just off Gray's Inn Road in Clerkenwell. During his three years at University College in Dublin he had lived in student accommodation on the edge of the city. Living on his own was quite a new experience. He found that doing his own shopping, cooking and taking his clothes to the launderette took up far more time than he could ever have imagined. But the upside was that he could walk to Lincoln's Inn Fields in less than ten minutes. His pupillage course consisted of lectures and individual instruction lasting no more than three or four hours a day. He was also required to attend court sessions, those at the Old Bailey being by far the most important - and the most interesting. So he had plenty of time to explore London.

Although the war had ended four years ago, it appeared that over half the city had been destroyed. Wherever the eye could see, there were bombed sites with huge holes full of weeds, rank grass and rubble. Rats ran around, proliferating at an alarming rate. To Liam it seemed that the vile destruction was due to six years of evil and hatred. The thought struck him that if Germany had defeated the Allies, the whole of the British Isles, including the Republic of Ireland, would have been ruled by a monstrous dictator and everyone would be speaking German. Liam had never met any Germans. He certainly didn't want to now.

To his surprise and relief, Liam realised he was better off financially than he had expected. He had a little bit extra that enabled him to visit museums, the theatre and dine in a modest restaurant once a week. One day, after spending a most absorbing and instructive morning at The Royal Courts of Justice on the Strand, he decided to take a walk down to Trafalgar Square. With a map of London now always at hand, he walked past Charing Cross Station and on to Trafalgar Square. Craning his neck to look up at the famous statue of Nelson, commemorating his victory at the Battle of Trafalgar in 1805, a restaurant on the corner of the Square caught his eye. He finished admiring the Nelson statue and crossed the busy road. There on the corner stood Lyons Corner House, with a large sign flashing on the front. And to ensure that passers-by hadn't missed the first sign, there was another similar one just inside the door. He went in and was shown to a table. There was plenty of choice on the menu, including a self-service salad bar, which could be visited as often as the diner wished. As he was finishing his meal, a piano trio started playing excerpts from music popular at the time, including *Guys and Dolls; I Leave My Heart in an English Garden; If I Knew You Were Coming I'd Have Baked a Cake; Marry the Man Today.* All the music was quite new to Liam, as he listened, entranced. After about fifteen minutes he felt he should let other diners use his table, so he called the waitress and paid the bill.

'Is there music each day at this time?' he enquired.

'Only on Fridays, Saturdays and Sundays. Friday and Saturday evenings are the best times. The trio plays from six until ten pm, with a half hour break.'

Liam thanked the waitress and vowed to return next week.

Lunching at Lyons Corner House on a Friday, Saturday or Sunday soon became a routine. Liam chose a table as near the platform as possible so he could both see and hear the players better. The group consisted of three performers: piano, violin and cello. In his complete ignorance of almost any music, light, jazz or classical, Liam had no idea that the group was called a piano trio. But he was learning fast. He discovered that jazz had a particular swinging dance-like rhythm; the few popular songs of the time that he recognised possessed a melodic intimacy. But it was the classical pieces that attracted him the most. He had never heard any Mozart, Haydn or Schubert, not even a Johann Strauss Waltz. But these composers soon became his favourites. The lilting melodies and harmonic sequences began to sing in his head long after he had actually heard them.

The trio consisted of two female performers and one male. The pianist and violinist were women, the cellist was male. It was the pianist who seemed to be in charge: a hand raised before the beginning of a piece, her head bobbing at the appropriate moment, and a bow at the end of a performance. As he became more and more absorbed, Liam asked a waitress if the trio had a title.

'I don't know. I'll ask.'

After a short break in the performance the waitress returned. 'It's called the *Trio Appassionata*.'

'Oh! Thank you.'

Liam thought quickly. Should he send a small 'thank you' payment via the waitress? Or would that be ungracious, perhaps even rude. Or should he send a note? A note saying what? He had absolutely no idea what the protocol was in this particular situation. And even the legal instruction in his pupillage training would be of no help whatsoever.

Giving a slight bow to the platform, he paid his bill and left the restaurant.

Liam's next visit to Lyons Corner House was on a Saturday evening just over a week later. To his delight there was a free table next to the platform. He sat down and studied the menu as the piano trio performed a trio by Mendelssohn. Liam had no idea what the music or the composer was, but he found it enchanting and totally absorbing.

The male cellist, earnest-looking, wearing heavily rimmed glasses, sat rather hunched up, scraping away, completely involved. His thick dark wavy hair was carefully combed back. Liam guessed he was in his early to mid-twenties. The female violinist sometimes played sitting down, sometimes standing up, which Liam found a little confusing. She was slim, with long straight fair hair, tied back in a ponytail, which bobbed around when the music was fast. She also performed with total involvement. Liam reckoned she was in the same age group as the cellist.

But it was the female pianist who Liam found the most appealing. The piano, being much larger than the two stringed instruments, was placed at the side of the platform, slightly further back from the audience. The lid was open half-way, facing the audience. The pianist sat on the left, so those seated on the left-hand side could watch as her hands floated around with rapid graceful movements. This view, absorbing although it was to Liam, meant he could only see the side of her face. As her hands flew up and down the keyboard, notes cascading forth, his urge to see her full on increased. The waitress arrived to take his order, but Liam was so absorbed in the music he didn't even notice her. He was trying to work out where he should place his chair so he could see the whole of the pianist's face. Success! Now he couldn't see her hands, but he could see her face. That is, unless she leant forward too far when it was obscured by the half-open piano lid. The waitress, non-plussed, moved away to take another order. The pianist, totally involved in performing, was unaware that a member of the audience was staring at her in complete absorption. Liam was enchanted by the perfectly oval face, slim dark eyebrows over well-spaced, deep-set eyes. He couldn't see the colour of her eyes from where he sat, but he imagined they were a deep blue. Her nose had a slightly upward turn, as if in the hope that her next meal would be really appetising. Her mouth was small and expressive. Liam sat on, entranced.

Finally the music stopped and the players stood up and bowed to indifferent applause. Oh, well, thought Liam, it's a restaurant, not a concert hall. People are here primarily to eat and the music is just a sideline. The string players put their instruments away in elegantly shaped wooden cases and they all gathered up their music. They must be about to have a break, thought Liam. The pianist had the most amount of music to collect, as unbeknown to Liam; the piano copies have all the other parts included. As she reached out to pick up the final bundle, she accidentally let some of it fall on the floor. Liam was up on the platform in an instant.

'Please allow me,' he said as he gathered up the fallen sheets. 'I've *so* enjoyed hearing you play. How long is your break?'

'Oh! How kind. Most of the diners don't even notice us. They're too busy eating. Our break is half an hour. But you'll have finished your dinner by then.'

'No. I don't think so. I haven't even ordered it yet.'

'I'll look out for you,' said the pianist as she finally left the platform.

Liam returned to his table and signalled to the waitress.

Chapter Two

It was the last day of term at Hemel Hempstead Grammar School. It was the day when Miss Hart, the headmistress, always took the assembly. On this very special day all those in the upper sixth who were leaving school, had their names read out, stating what further education, if any, they were planning. As there were less than twenty-five girls leaving, this did not take as long as might have been expected. Assemblies took place in the gym. The pupils all sat on the floor, except for the sixth form, who were sufficiently privileged to be allowed to sit on chairs. The pupils' names were read out in alphabetical order.

'Angela Armstrong is going on to secretarial college.

'Bridget Boland is going to study nursing at St. Mary's Hospital in London.

'Carol Crab is going on to secretarial college.

'Doreen Dempsey has been offered a place at Magdalene College Oxford, depending on her A Level results.

'Emily Edwards is going to finishing school in Switzerland.

'Frances Fitch is going on to secretarial college.'

And so the list went on and on. Claire Tebbit stared out of the window, trying to concentrate. She knew all of the girls well and many were good friends. Most of them had been at the school together for seven years. The majority of them were going on to secretarial college, but there was a total of six girls going on to university. They had now arrived at the Ss. T was next so Claire stopped staring out of the window and looked straight ahead.

'Claire Tebbit has won a scholarship to the Royal Academy of Music in London.'

They had almost arrived at the end now. 'And Zoë Zedbetter is going on to study nursing.'

Applause broke out and many of the girls hugged each other. After a few seconds Miss Hart raised her hand for silence.

'I'd like to congratulate everyone who is going on to further study. And I would particularly like to congratulate those who have been offered university places and Claire Tebbit, who has done us all proud at Hemel Hempstead Grammar School with her scholarship to The Royal Academy of Music in London.'

'Congratulations again, darling. And how did it go?'

'It went very well, thank you, Mummy. I was the only one to win a scholarship, but six girls are going on to uni provided their A Level results are good enough. How's Dad?'

'He's resting after his chemo session. But hopefully he'll be up for dinner.'

'I hope so too. Above all, let's hope the chemotherapy works.'

'I'm sure it will.'

Gwen Tebbit looked strained and anxious. Her husband, Clive had developed prostate cancer a year ago and was finding chemotherapy a big struggle. Gwen, now her husband's main carer, was also finding life a struggle. Although Clive was sixteen years her senior, she hadn't expected him to fall seriously ill at the age of only fifty-nine.

Claire was more than relieved when her parents agreed that she should find 'digs' somewhere in North London near the Royal Academy of Music in Marylebone Road. Of course the area was far too expensive for students to live in, but with the help of the student advisory department, she found a room with a family off Kilburn High Road. The room was extremely small, the house was cold and the meals, included in the very reasonable cost, were poor. But the upside was that there was a piano, which Claire could play as much as she wished at a small additional charge. And in an hour she could be back in Hemel Hempstead for a decent meal. Her timetable at the RAM was limited, to say the least. She had a one hour individual piano lesson each week with her piano professor and a half hour composition lesson with one of the Academy's leading composition professors. There was a history of music lecture, a harmony class and a compulsory two hour choir practice. The classes and lectures were spread over two and a half days, which left her a great deal of time to practice the piano. The total number of individual classes and lectures each week added up to only five and a half hours. This meant that all the students spent most of the week on their own. Self-motivation was of prime importance.

The social hub at the Royal Academy of Music was the canteen. Situated in the basement of the large, handsome Baroque-style building, it was never less than half full. Most of the students had lunch there on the day of their class or course. The food wasn't exactly gourmet standard, but it was mostly edible, and extremely cheap. Students in different year levels chatted over coffee and snacks and friendships were made. Some formed professional partnerships, which lasted for many years. There were also many hangers-on, known as the 'canteen proppers.' These were mainly students studying singing. Their explanation was that the human voice should never be over-exposed; therefore their practice time was, of necessity, strictly limited. The instrumental students regarded the singers as having little talent and no motivation, who relied on the acquaintance of the more gifted students to keep them 'on course', at least socially, if not musically.

There was a notice board, placed prominently by the entrance in the corridor so that no one could miss it. There were two sections, one covering property 'lost and found,' the other concerning students seeking others in the hope of establishing a musical partnership. By the beginning of her second week Claire glanced at it each time she went into the canteen. Some of the items were amusing, others quite serious.

Lost and Found

Found: a pair of gentleman's leather gloves with a hole in the left thumb.
Found: a lady's right high-heeled shoe with the heel missing.
Lost: a violin bow in good condition.

Lost: a leather case containing six new hand-made oboe reeds.

Then came the more serious items.
String quartet seeks viola player of high standard.
French horn player seeks position in wind quintet.
Pianist wanted to form a piano trio. Must be of high standard and a very good sight-reader.

All the announcements included phone numbers.

Claire scribbled down the phone number of *Pianist wanted to form a piano trio*, consumed a barely edible lunch and went to her harmony class. Later that evening she asked her landlady if she could make a phone call. Use of the phone was strictly limited. Every second was charged, with a bit extra added on for 'the inconvenience.' A male voice answered.

'Hello? Who is it, please?'

'I'm Claire Tebbit. I'm calling in answer to your advertisement on the RAM notice board requesting a pianist for your piano trio.'

'Oh, yes. Are you a student at the RAM?'

'Yes, indeed.'

'What year are you in?'

'First year.'

'Oh. Is that all? Sarah and I are in our third.'

'Does that matter?'

'I suppose not. Will you come and play to us? I'm the cellist and my name is Charles Boland. The violinist's name is Sarah Unwin.'

Charles gave Claire an address not far from Kilburn High Road and a date was arranged.

Claire arrived at the appointed time, well provided with music, including two Mozart Piano Trios she had been working on. Struggling up eight flights of steep, narrow stairs, she reached the top of the house. In the open doorway stood a young man with dark hair and thick glasses, aged about twenty, whom Claire assumed was the cellist, Charles Boland. He shook her hand warmly.

'Claire Tebbit? I'm so sorry about all the stairs. It's the only reasonably priced place I could find that would allow the practice of musical instruments. Do sit down. May I introduce Sarah Unwin, my violinist?'

Claire shook hands with a tall slim young lady with long fair hair tied back in a ponytail. She was very attractive, also aged about twenty. Claire thought it wiser to ignore Charles's description of her as 'my violinist.'

'I'll get straight to the point,' said Charles. 'Sarah and I have always wanted to play chamber music professionally. We feel too anonymous in an orchestra. We're both doing a four-year course, so we have another year in hand. Rather than forming a string quartet, we thought we'd start off with a piano trio, which we could expand at any time. There are so many major works written for different instrumental combinations as well as the string quartet, as I'm sure you know.'

Claire nodded.

'We'll draw up a list of piano trios, which appeal most to the three of us. But first I have a bit of a surprise, which I hope will appeal to you. If not, we'll work out something else. I don't know how well off you are financially, and of course I wouldn't dream of asking. But most students, you'll probably agree, tend to be down on their uppers.'

Claire nodded again. 'I agree entirely.'

'So this is an idea for making money – hopefully easy money.'

Charles paused for effect and then continued. 'I happen to know the manager of Lyons Corner House. It's a large restaurant cum café on the corner of Trafalgar Square. Do you know it?'

'I've walked past it but I've never been in.'

'It's quite impressive and considering we're still being rationed, the food is better than average. The manager is a family friend. When he dined at my parents' house recently he explained his new idea, which is to have light music performed at lunchtime and perhaps in the evening, just at weekends, to entice more diners. He actually suggested a piano trio rather than a string quartet and asked me if I could organise it. That's why you're here.'

Claire was rather at a loss. It was not at all what she had expected.

'I'll have to think about it. I was expecting – well – Mozart and Beethoven piano trios... What sort of music were you thinking of? I don't know anything about pop – or any light music. I'm really only interested in classical music.'

'Yes, of course. I quite understand that. But what about musicals? That's more what we were thinking of, wasn't it Sarah? And of course we could include some classical movements as well. It's always good to try and educate the public, isn't it?' He gave a mirthless little laugh. 'But before we go any further, perhaps you'd like to play to us?'

'Of course.' Claire rustled around in her music case and took out a couple of sheets. What should it be? She had been planning to play Beethoven's *Pathétique*

Sonata, but now she realised it might be too serious for this rather unusual occasion. She sat down at the piano, a rather shabby little upright, obviously old, with candlestick holders on either side.

'I'll start with Chopin,' she said and launched into the well-known Waltz in E Flat Opus 18. Charles and Sarah clapped enthusiastically.

'Excellent,' said Charles. 'Beautifully executed and very musical. Anything else? Perhaps as a contrast?'

Claire had also thought of a contrast and played Schubert's Impromptu in G Flat Major Deutsch 899 No 3.

After more enthusiastic applause, Charles said: 'well, hopefully, I think our piano trio is formed. We'll have to think of a good name. But now I'd like to invite both you ladies out to lunch at the Lyons Corner House near Trafalgar Square. My friend, the manager is expecting us and has reserved a table. We'll be there in about half an hour. It's just beside the tube station.'

The piano trio became the *Trio Appassionata* and met two evenings a week to select the music they would play at Lyons Corner House. They all agreed on a varied programme: well-known themes from present day musicals and some light-weight jazz interspersed with single movements from trios by Mozart, Beethoven, Mendelssohn, Schubert and other well-known classical composers. As Charles had remarked at their original meeting: 'it's always good to try and educate the public.'

They didn't always keep to the trio format. Sometimes they played works for violin and piano, cello and piano and the odd solo piece.

On a Saturday in early December the great day arrived. The small concert platform had been carefully set out by the management and promptly at six o'clock, the three musicians walked onto the stage complete with music, the string players carrying their instruments. None of the diners took the least bit of notice. Accustomed as they were to some applause on their entrance, the performers felt a little disconcerted. The two string players had already tuned up off-stage, so once they had settled down and placed the selected music on the music stands, Claire raised her hand, gave a little nod and they launched into a number of the musical *Salad Days,* extremely popular at the time.

They all thought the performance had gone well, but again the diners took no notice whatsoever. Knives and forks clattered and the conversation seemed to get louder. There was no applause.

The trio soldiered on until ten o'clock with a half hour break. At the end of their stalwart performance they were pleased to receive their payment and relieved that they had a break for almost a week. This pattern continued until the end of June, when Claire accidentally let her music drop on the floor as they were tidying up. To her surprise a young male diner jumped onto the platform, picked up the music and handed it back to her.

Chapter Three

At the weekends Liam lunched and dined at Lyons Corner House as often as he could afford to. He selected a table close to the platform, whenever one was available, positioning his chair so that he could see the pianist. Of course, he always hoped that she would also see him. By the end of the third week he persuaded the waitress to give her a note in the trio's break time. The note was brief and to the point.

Dear Piano Player,

I don't know whether you remember that about three weeks ago I picked up the music, which you had accidentally dropped on the platform. Since then I have been lunching or dining here as often as I can afford to in the hope of possibly meeting you. I do so enjoy your excellent playing and the music too. Perhaps we could meet up after one of your lunchtime concerts?

Best regards, Liam O'Malley.

His telephone number was included.

For Liam the next two weeks passed in semi-frenzy. He wasn't always able to get a table next to the platform and twice he was forced to sit at the back of the restaurant. Then one Saturday lunchtime his luck turned. He was ushered to a table right by the platform, slightly to the left. He could see the side of the pianist's face and if he leant forward a little he could see more of her. He barely tasted what he was eating and he hoped, desperately hoped that she would notice him. When the musicians' break came Liam half stood up. Please, please notice me, he kept saying to himself. The pianist stood up and collected some music off the stand. Please drop it, thought Liam. She didn't. But she noticed him and raised her hand slightly. In an instant Liam was up on the platform and extended his hand.

'I'm Liam O'Malley. A few weeks ago I wrote you a note. Perhaps we could meet up for lunch? On a day when you're not playing here?'

'I'm free tomorrow,' the young lady replied. 'I'm Claire Tebbit. I'll give you my phone number.'

The following day, as arranged, Liam met Claire by Nelson's statue in Trafalgar Square. He had selected a meeting place known to both of them, but he didn't expect that Claire would want to lunch at Lyons Corner House. It was, after all, her work place. Fortunately for Liam, Claire knew London well and they walked the short distance to Leicester Square.

As Liam had hoped, the lunch was a huge success. Lunch turned into dinner and soon they were meeting three or four times a week. Two months later Liam realised he was in love with Claire. He wanted to be with her always, forever and possess her utterly. Unfortunately for Liam, in the early 1950s, respectable unmarried 'middle class' couples did not tumble into bed together, however much they were in love. Liam was aware of this and realised he would have to bide his time. He knew that marriage was the only option, but was it too soon? They had met briefly for the first time six months ago and had been an 'item' only for the last two. How long should he wait before he proposed marriage?

Then there were practical problems. Money, or lack of it, was the biggest hurdle. Where would they live? What would they live on? The other problem was religion. Liam was a Roman Catholic. Claire was not. Liam was too nervous to bring up the question of religion. How should he start? What should he say? Then the added problem was his Irish background. How could any woman coming from a London suburb, even as undistinguished as Hemel Hempstead, consider marrying a man from Westport in County Mayo?

Then a very sad event occurred, which put Liam's marriage proposal on hold. Claire's father, Clive Tebbit died on his sixtieth birthday, 31st March 1950. Although his death had been expected and fully predicted by the medical profession, Gwen, his wife was overwhelmed with grief. Aged only forty-four, it was not how she imagined her life would turn out. She felt isolated and totally abandoned and turned to Claire for help and support. Claire realised she had no alternative but to give up her digs near Kilburn High Road and move back to Hemel Hempstead to take care of her mother.

'I'm really sorry,' Claire explained when her landlady objected to the short notice. 'I'd much rather live here during term time. It's much easier to get to the Academy from here than from my mother's home in Hemel Hempstead. But don't worry; I'm sure the office will find you another student. In the meantime I'll give you a month's rent in advance.'

Claire was now beginning to find the five weekend performances with the *Trio Appassionata* at Lyons Corner House an increasing strain. Even before the death of her father she had found the sessions draining. It wasn't only the light numbers, which she found pointless and boring; it was more the attitude of the diners. The performers' arrival on the platform was never acknowledged and there was almost no applause when they had finished playing a piece, even a well-known popular item. Also, their financial remuneration remained the same.

Claire had, of course, told her fellow musicians about her father's death. Both were extremely sympathetic, but there was no mention of giving fewer performances.

Then one evening as they were packing up in the green room, Charles, the cellist persuaded them to stay on for a brief chat.

'I don't know how you ladies feel, but I am finding it increasingly difficult to continue performing under these circumstances. The diners take almost no notice of us and we are paid a pittance. Should we give in our notice right away? Or do you both need the money, little though it is?'

Both ladies raised their eyebrows in surprise. Neither of them had expected a musician of Charles's stature to give up so easily. It was Claire, relief welling up inside, who spoke first.

'I see your point, Charles. We are short-changed by the management – *and* the diners. It would certainly help my problems looking after my widowed mother not to come here on weekend evenings. As you can imagine, the journey back to Hemel Hempstead at ten o'clock at night is no joke. However, should we give it all up? What about just doing lunches at weekends? We could play from midday to two o'clock on Saturdays and Sundays. Perhaps even on Fridays as well. But I agree entirely about the money. Negotiate the hours and the money, Charles. If that works we could put up with lack of interest from the diners. Should we think it over and talk again tomorrow?'

'Well spoken, Claire,' said Sarah. 'I don't think we should rush into any resignations – yet. What do you think, Charles?'

'I'll have to go along with you two.' Charles placed his cello carefully in the case and clicked the lid shut. 'Let's talk again tomorrow.'

Clive Tebbit's funeral the following week was a strained and dismal affair. His two sons, who had both emigrated to Canada and Australia six years ago, flew over to attend their father's funeral. But they were unable to help with the organisation, which, Claire discovered to her dismay, was left entirely up to her. A few days later Claire's brothers returned to their newly adopted countries while Claire was left in charge of looking after her distraught mother. All she had to look forward to now, or so she thought, was the start of the new summer term at the Academy in three weeks time.

But she had reckoned without Liam. When Claire had called Liam to tell him about her father's death and her mother's distress, he offered to come round to the house in Hemel Hempstead.

'I could shop for you and do some cooking and cleaning. I want to see you, Claire, and help in any way I can.'

After two weeks of Liam's pleading Claire gave in. She wanted to see him too. Finally, she invited him to lunch.

'Mummy, I have a friend I would like you to meet. He's coming to lunch tomorrow.'

'He? You mean you have a boyfriend?'

'Well, I suppose that's one way of putting it.'

Liam arrived promptly on time, armed with a bottle of champagne. A little later, when Gwen was busy in the kitchen, he knelt down in front of Claire's chair and took both her hands.

'Darling, Claire, I love you so much. Please will you marry me?'

Returning to announce that lunch was ready, Gwen found them locked in a passionate embrace.

Chapter Four

'He's not English, is he Claire? He has a slightly different accent to English people.'

'No, he's not English, Mummy. He's from Ireland.'

'*Ireland!* That's unusual. What part of Ireland? Dublin?'

'No. He's from Westport, County Mayo.'

'Where's that? I've never heard of it.'

'It's in the West of Ireland. Near Connemara.'

'I've never heard of Connemara either. Is that where you will live when you're married?'

'No, Mummy. We'll be living in London. Liam has no plans to return to his home town. He finds it too isolated. And he's enjoying London now.'

'Especially as he's met you, I suppose. Have you planned a date for the wedding?'

'We're thinking of next April.'

'That's only four months away.'

'Yes. I know. But it'll be a small wedding.'

'Here in our local church, I hope.'

'Probably not, Mummy. As Liam's a Roman Catholic it'll probably be in the local registry office.'

'He's a *Roman Catholic!*'

'Yes, Mummy. But it's just another form of Christianity.'

Gwen clucked, but said nothing more.

In April 1951 Claire and Liam had a simple wedding at the local registry office in Hemel Hempstead with twenty-five guests. As Claire's brothers were unable to travel from Canada and Australia so soon after their father's funeral, Charles, the cellist gave Claire away. Liam invited his family from Westport but none of them was able to attend. They sent their excuses. It was too far to travel; the journey was too expensive; they couldn't get time off work.

Gwen put a brave face on the fact that she had now lost her only daughter – to an Irish Roman Catholic.

Liam finished his lawyers' pupillage course in Lincoln's Inn Fields, attaining a top grade. Claire finished her course at the Royal Academy of Music, also with a top grade. They were now both about to start off together on Life's Great Journey. All that remained was to find somewhere suitable to live, preferably larger than Liam's one bedroom flat off Gray's Inn Road. But they felt there was no rush to find a larger property. They were wildly, madly in love. The world was their oyster and they had everything to live for.

Liam pulled down the sheet and gently stroked her stomach. Claire gave a voluptuous sigh.

'Don't stop. Just stroke me further down.'

Liam moved his hand down her slim smooth thigh. 'Don't worry. I've barely started yet.'

Liam continued stroking as Claire gave a little moan. She reached for his groin, feeling him shudder as she gently squeezed and stroked his penis. In less than a minute he had mounted her and came to his climax with a joyful shout. He kissed her gently on the mouth, lay back and fell fast asleep. Claire got up quietly and went into the bathroom. She ran a small bath and washed out her vagina. This was not the right time for a pregnancy, certainly not for her. She crept back to bed and slipped in beside her husband.

Liam came into the dining-kitchen, formally dressed in a dark suit, waistcoat and sober tie. Claire smiled up at him from where she sat at the table reading *The Times,* which was delivered to their London flat every morning.

'Impeccably dressed for one of the most important days in your legal career,' she remarked. 'Ready for coffee?'

'Please. Yes, it's been several weeks of preparation for this very important case. At the Old Bailey, as you know.'

'I've been watching you work on it. It's quite a big step up to be part of the prosecuting council so early in your career.'

'It is. Even though I'm the most junior.' Liam tucked into his fresh toast. 'And what are your plans for today, darling?'

'Well, as it's my weekly day off school I haven't completely made up my mind yet. But I'll spend at least three or four hours on the piano. We have a concert coming up in four weeks.'

'Where is the concert?'

'In the Harrogate Town Hall.'

'Is that a step in the right direction?'

'Definitely.'

Liam stood up, ready to leave. Claire followed him to the front door and they exchanged a fond farewell kiss. As she washed up the dishes Claire had to decide which piece to work on first, the Beethoven or the Mozart?

Probably the Beethoven. It was far more technically challenging and more tiring. But first she had to get through scales, arpeggios and some exercises. Luckily she had a good system. A different key for each day worked out in a chromatic sequence. Today's key was A flat: most appropriate for Beethoven. She washed and dressed hastily and was sitting at the piano within ten minutes.

Liam returned home in the evening in a rather subdued mood.

'Did it go well?' enquired Claire.

'I wouldn't describe it as "going well." The case is too depressing to say anything good about it. But it is progressing. The unfortunate victim sits in the dock sobbing a great deal of the time.'

'That must be most distressing.'

'It is. And a lot of the female jurors cry too.'

'That must be awful. What's the ratio of male to female jurors?'

'Seven men to five women.'

'I think you need a stiff drink. Gin and tonic or chilled Chablis?'

'A G&T sounds good.'

Claire got up to pour the drinks, giving Liam a light kiss on the forehead as she passed.

'When I've had the G&T I'll have a wash and change.'

Liam's harrowing case at the Old Bailey continued for two weeks. Each day he came home looking more and more exhausted.

'The jury will probably go out today around midday,' he explained at breakfast, unable to eat anything.

'I'm sure it'll be the verdict you all want.' Claire lifted up the coffee pot.

'No, thanks. I have to leave early to go through my brief again.'

When Liam returned home that evening he looked absolutely drained and his face had a slightly grey tinge. Claire knew the news was bad but was too afraid to ask. Liam pulled off his jacket, waistcoat and tie and sat down heavily on the sofa.

'G&T?'

'Yes, a double please, darling – then I'm going to bed.'

Claire refrained from saying that she had just cooked one of his favourite meals. 'What was the verdict?'

'The rapist got off with a caution.'

'A *caution!* Is that all? Why?'

'He persuaded the jury that the victim had encouraged him.'

'How appalling.'

'It was.'

Liam slept through the night, barely moving. The following morning he took Claire in his arms. 'I need a break.'

'Of course. What kind of a break?'

'I'd like to go away on holiday.'

'Where to?'

'Achill Island.'

'Near where you were brought up?'

'Yes, quite near. We could visit my family in Westport, where I was born.'

'Could you wait till my concert is over?'

'Of course, darling. When is it?'

'Saturday 20 June.'

'In the Harrogate Town Hall?'

'Yes.'

'Certainly. That's less than ten days away. It'll take me that long to arrange it all.'

Claire's concert in the Harrogate Town Hall was a huge success and received rave reviews in the local press.

The Appassionata Piano Trio from London gave excellent performances of the Haydn Piano Trio No:39 in G major; Schubert's Piano Trio No: 2 in E Flat; ending with Beethoven's Archduke Trio in B Flat Opus 97. The two string players showed great flair and musicianship, but it was the pianist, Claire Tebbit, who supplied the inspiration.

Claire was absolutely delighted and Liam was extremely proud of his wife. The success of the concert augured well for their trip to Achill Island.

On 1st July they flew to Shannon Airport, where Liam had arranged a self-drive hire car.

'There's little or no public transport in the Irish countryside.' he explained. 'We need to be able to get around on our own.'

It was Claire's first visit to the Republic of Ireland and she had no idea what to expect. As Liam drove out of Shannon Airport, Claire noticed a road sign to Killarney.

'Killarney! I've heard of Killarney! Apparently it's very beautiful. Is that where we're going?'

Liam laughed. 'I'm afraid not. We're going in the opposite direction. Killarney's in County Kerry, in the southernmost part of Ireland. We're going to the most westerly point. But first we pass through Galway Town, where I though we'd have a late lunch.'

He followed a sign for Ennis and they drove in silence for a while. The sign for Ennis came up on the signboard in two languages, English being the lower one.

'What's the first language?' enquired Claire.

'Irish Gaelic.'

This was a surprise to Claire. 'Does everyone speak Gaelic? Don't they speak English?'

Liam laughed. 'Hardly anyone in Ireland speaks Gaelic now.' He stroked her knee. 'Don't worry, darling. You won't have to learn Gaelic. You probably won't even hear it unless we go to the Gaeltacht, a very small area in County Galway. It's a bit of a detour so we won't do it today. But another day... if you'd like to...' He looked doubtfully at his wife.

'Let's wait and see, shall we? I certainly have a lot of new things to get my head around. Is there a great difference between Catholics and Protestants in Ireland?'

'Oh, yes!' Liam gave a harsh little laugh. 'After the Reformation the British made sure that the Protestants got all the top perks. They confiscated the majority of the Catholic-owned land and gave it to the British, who were almost all Protestants. Hence the term Anglo-Irish. And although they make up only 5% of the population, the Protestants still own most of the land and have most of the top jobs in industry.'

'I've never noticed any lack of harmony between Catholics and Protestants in England,' remarked Claire. 'Especially in London.'

'But London is probably one of the most cosmopolitan and tolerant cities in the world. Even now in the 1950s.'

'What about your family here in Westport? Are they tolerant of Protestants? Do they know you've married one?'

'Oh, yes. They know I've married a Protestant.'

'And what do they think?'

'Well, when they meet you, they will like you so much it won't make any difference.' Claire wasn't so sure. It was the first time in her life that religion had raised its ugly head.

Forty-five minutes later the sign to Galway Town appeared, the Gaelic above with the English below.

'Is this an important town?'

'Well, it's the capital of County Galway. So it is important.'

Liam found a parking space next to a pub called The Galway Arms.

'The name seems rather appropriate,' he said, reversing expertly into the small space. 'Let's go in.'

He opened the passenger door for Claire, who got out slowly, wondering what new challenge awaited her. Liam led the way to the pub door, stepping back to let Claire lead the way.

'Your first visit to an Irish pub.'

Claire looked into the dark, heavily beamed interior, a fire burning in the grate. Well, here we go, she thought.

The lunch was a great deal better than they had expected, but Liam didn't want to linger. He remembered that the further west one travelled the worse the roads became. None of the roads on Achill Island were surfaced and some were very treacherous. He had informed the hotel landlord that they would arrive before nine pm, as he didn't want to drive on treacherous roads in the dark. Ten minutes later Claire was fast asleep. Liam was glad he had suggested she have a glass of wine, although he didn't dare have one himself. He was now driving northwest towards Letterfrack, along the shores of Lough Corrib, shimmering, grey and faceless in the fading light. Soon they were driving through 'Joyce Country.' He wondered if Claire had read any James Joyce. Should he ask her over dinner? Then the sign to Westport appeared. My birthplace, thought Liam. Where I grew up. Should I stop and have a look? No, it's better to drive on. If I stopped, Claire might wake up. It was a good half hour to Achill Island now, depending on the conditions of the roads. It had begun to rain. Not heavily, just thin mizzling rain, more like a mist. That was the norm in County Mayo, even in July and August and reminded Liam of his childhood.

The rain was becoming heavier now. Liam realised he must stop reminiscing about his childhood and concentrate on the present challenges on the road ahead. At ten minutes to nine he pulled the car off the road onto the rough unsurfaced drive of the Achill Head Hotel. The jolting woke Claire.

'Where are we?'

'We've arrived at our final destination, the Achill Head Hotel, where I'm sure we'll spend a most enjoyable holiday.'

Claire opened her eyes in surprise, but she didn't really like what she saw.

Their bedroom was up two steep flights of stairs and faced the sea, although it was already too dark to see the view. That would have to wait until the morning. The room was quite large but rather bare. There was no carpet, just uneven floorboards with a scudded surface. The bed was a standard-size double, smaller than Liam and Claire were accustomed to. There were scruffy bedside tables on either side, their surfaces resembling the floor. The dark wardrobe, full of cracks, leant forward at a dangerous angle. The bathroom was along the corridor and had to be shared with two other guests. Fortunately for Liam and Claire the hotel was almost empty and they had the bathroom to themselves.

Claire sat down on the bed, which creaked. It was hard and unyielding.

'Did you actually stay here?' she enquired.

Liam sat down beside her on the bed. 'No. We lunched here when I was about eleven. I loved it. Sadly, Dad thought it was too expensive. But I thought we'd give it a try. A new Irish experience for both of us.'

He stood up. 'Let's go down to the restaurant. They've promised to serve us a cold supper.'

The restaurant was cheerless and completely empty. On one of the tables were two plates of cold food – mostly meat.

'I'll order a bottle of wine,' said Liam. He called out as pleasantly as possible: 'excuse me – is anyone there?'

A few minutes later a waiter appeared, not particularly smartly dressed.

'May I have the wine list, please?' enquired Liam.

'Sorry, sir. The bar's closed. It's after nine o'clock.'

Despite the hard creaking bed and the disappointment over the lack of wine, they both slept soundly and didn't wake up until after ten o'clock. Claire got up first and opened the curtains. The rain was pouring down and a heavy mist completely obscured any possible view.

'It's raining,' she remarked, quite unnecessarily. 'Does it rain a lot here?'

'It does sometimes but I'm sure it'll clear up later and we can go for a drive. Let's dress and see if we can persuade the management to give us some breakfast.'

'Room service?' suggested Claire.

'I doubt it. I think we should dress and go downstairs.'

Fifteen minutes later they were down in the restaurant, again completely empty. The same badly dressed waiter as the night before appeared and came up to their empty unlaid table. 'Sorry, sir, madam, breakfast finished at nine thirty.'

'Would it be possible to have some coffee?' enquired Liam. 'Instant will do.'

'I'll see,' said the waiter and sloped off towards the kitchen. He returned ten minutes later with two cups, the liquid slurping into the saucers.

'Thank you,' said Liam. 'What time is lunch?'

'Twelve thirty until two. The kitchen closes at one thirty.'

'Well, we've certainly arrived in a different world,' remarked Claire. 'What shall we do until twelve thirty? It's still chucking it down out there.'

'Explore the hotel? There's not much else we can do.'

Of course the bar was closed, but they found the lounge without difficulty. It was a large room, sparsely furnished with an uneven scuffed wooden floor, similar to that in their bedroom, covered with half a dozen or so shabby rugs. In one corner stood a baby grand piano.

'Claire! There's a piano!'

Claire walked over to it, expecting it to be locked, but she lifted the lid of the keyboard with ease. Sitting down on the stool, she adjusted it to a suitable height and began to play Chopin's *Polonaise Fantasie* Opus 61 in A flat.

Liam sat down on a sofa and listened, entranced. His wife was certainly an exceptionally good pianist. Suddenly something crashed in the nearby kitchen and the unkempt waiter appeared at the lounge door. Liam raised his hand for silence and the waiter, getting the message, leant against the door until Claire had finished. Then he clapped with great enthusiasm.

'Madam, you really *are* some pianist.'

'Thank you,' said Claire, and launched into a Liszt *Hungarian Rhapsody* .

Lunch was much better than they had expected and surprise, surprise, the bar was open, so they enjoyed a rather good bottle of *Fleurie*. They spent the afternoon in bed, making love and sleeping.

The next two days were spent in exactly the same manner, with one exception; they alarmed for nine am and just made it to breakfast in time. Rather to Liam's surprise, Claire had brought some music with her and sat down to play after breakfast.

After the first piece had ended, Liam enquired what it was.

'The 1st movement of the Brahms Sonata in A major for Violin and Piano. I'm just playing the piano part.'

'Of course. Who'll play the violin part?'

'The violin in my piano trio.'

'Oh! What will the third player do?'

'Just sit and listen until his turn comes to play something else.'

'Oh, I see,' said Liam, but he didn't.

On the fourth day the sun came out. As she opened the curtains, Claire gasped with delight as she looked out onto the Atlantic Ocean, the light rippling waves gleaming like sparklers.

'Liam! Quick! Come and look before the sun goes in!'

He joined her at the window, crowing with delight. They were in the car shortly after ten o'clock, complete with a picnic lunch. The shabby waiter had grumbled at their request: 'it's not the usual procedure, sir.'

'But we're paying for lunch anyway,' Liam objected. 'I'm sure it won't take you that long to make up a few sandwiches.'

As the picnic was presented in a rather attractive wicker basket, Liam felt sure this was not a 'first.' They drove down towards the beach on the route they had taken to the hotel the day they arrived. Liam parked the car on a firm shingly section next to a battered sign saying: CAR PA... There was no one in sight. The sun shone down from an almost cloudless blue sky and a slight westerly wind blew in from the Atlantic Ocean, rippling up in small waves. The long wide beach stretched in both directions into infinity and the view was quite stunning. Claire gave a gasp of delight.

'It's quite beautiful!'

'The beach is called Keel Strand,' explained Liam. 'Fancy a little walk along the shore?'

'Yes. Why not? Shoes on or off?'

'Let's take them off. Then we can have a paddle.'

'Is that what you did when you were a boy?'

'My brother, Dermot and I used to swim here when we were boys. We even swam when it was raining. Then by the time I was fourteen and my brother was sixteen Dad gave us driving lessons along the beach.'

'Good Lord! Miles of space but no traffic to battle with.'

'I think that was the point. So we could get used to the mechanics of driving without the danger of hitting anything.'

'And that came later, I suppose.'

Liam gave Claire a hug. 'No, I've never hit anything – yet.'

'So the next bit of land is America,' remarked Claire.

Liam laughed. 'A long way off. About three thousand miles.'

'Three or four days by boat?'

'Probably – depending on the size of the boat.'

They had now reached the water's edge. Claire tied the laces of her shoes together, hung them around her neck and rolled up her trousers.

'C'mon, Liam! Let's go for a paddle.'

Liam followed Claire's example and they stepped gingerly into the water. They were a striking couple. At just over six feet tall, Liam had broad shoulders and slim hips. He had dark brown hair and brown eyes, a high forehead and an aquiline nose. Claire was of slight build, five feet five inches tall, with dark wavy hair and blue eyes. They played together almost like children and were obviously very much in love.

'The water's not as cold as I thought it would be,' said Claire.

'Want to go back for your swimsuit?' asked Liam, teasingly.

'Perhaps tomorrow. Oh, look!' said Claire, pointing out to sea. 'Talking of boats: there's one out there coming towards us.'

'Oh, yes! Liam's gaze followed her outstretched hand. 'Yes, it *is* coming this way. But it's pretty small. It wouldn't take us to America.' He shielded his eyes from the sun. 'It's a small fishing boat called a currach. Fancy a fishing trip?'

'Not really. You know I'm a poor swimmer.'

Liam laughed. 'I don't think swimming ability would affect a fishing expedition. I used to go out with the fishermen when I was a kid. Mackerel was their main catch. Like mackerel?'

'I don't think I've ever tried it.'

'I'll ask our scruffy waiter tonight if there's any chance of having some. Shall we go back to the car and drive on? You've hardly seen anything yet. I've planned a really lovely spot for our picnic lunch.'

Back at the car, they dried off and put on their shoes and socks. Once out on the narrow unsurfaced road, Liam turned left, passing the Achill Head Hotel on the right. The road narrowed into a track, becoming more and more bumpy. To the left it sheered away down a steep cliff towards the Atlantic. On the right another cliff appeared, almost straight up, covered with wire netting to prevent the stones from falling onto the road. They were going steadily uphill.

'I hope we don't meet another car,' said Claire with some feeling.

'Or a farm vehicle.'

'What happens if we do?'

'One of us has to reverse.'

They made it to the top without any mishap and Liam stopped in a small parking space.

'Look down there, Claire. Isn't that lovely? It's Keem Bay.'

Claire looked down at the small cove below them, surrounded by cliffs with the sea curving into it. It was magical.

'I'm going to drive down so we can have our picnic on the seashore.'

The picnic was a great deal better than either of them had expected. The hotel had even supplied a rug and two bottles of beer.

'I'll have to thank our waiter and give him a tip,' said Liam, throwing the leftovers to the gulls circling overhead.

Their picnic finished, they lay back on the sand to relax and digest. Claire dozed off as Liam looked out to sea, admiring it all: the view, the peace, and the silence. Suddenly he heard the sound of an outboard engine and a small currach came into view. I wonder if it's going to land here, he thought. I'd love to go out fishing. Maybe I'll suggest to Claire that I go out on my own while she's resting or playing the piano. Even a couple of hours would be great. The currach came close to the shore, as if the sailors were making an inspection, then turned round and went out to sea.

Liam and Claire drove back to the hotel in companionable silence.

'I've arranged that we visit my family on Thursday.'

'Oh, good. For lunch?'

'Yes. I said we'd arrive about twelve thirty. I suggested I take everyone out. It'll make a change for them.'

'Of course. How did you get in touch? By phone?'

'No. They don't have a telephone. I sent a telegram from the hotel.'

'Goodness me! Imagine living without a telephone in 1954!'

'Yes, it does seem incredibly backward to us Londoners. But the West of Ireland has never been particularly advanced by any British or European standards. It's almost like the Third World.'

Claire wondered how she would get on with Liam's family. She didn't even know their names. Time for that later. Of course she and Liam had invited them to their wedding three years ago, but they all gave different excuses as to why they were unable to attend. Liam was less upset about their refusals than she had expected. Perhaps he wasn't close to his family? She didn't feel she should enquire. In just a few days time she would meet them. At that point on their holiday Claire had no idea under what circumstances she would finally meet Liam's family.

'Will you come to Mass with me this morning?'

'*Mass!* Do you mean Roman Catholic Mass?'

'Yes. Of course. There isn't any other form of Mass that I'm aware of.'

'But I'm not a Roman Catholic,' objected Claire.

'You're married to one.'

'Y-yes. I know. But...but you've never suggested my going to Mass before.'

The waiter collected their barely finished breakfast plates. 'More coffee, sir?'

'Oh, yes please. Could you heat it up a little?'

'I'll make fresh coffee if you like, sir.'

Fresh Nescafé, thought Claire.

'Yes, I'll come if you'd like me to, of course. What do I wear?'

'Just what you're wearing now. But wear a headscarf.'

It took a good half hour to reach the Catholic Church in Westport, on the mainland. The Church was small, smelt heavily of incense and was lit entirely by candlelight. Liam crossed himself and knelt down to pray, crossing himself again as he sat down beside Claire on the hard wooden pew. Claire sat and stared straight ahead. Slowly, they were joined by more members of the congregation, country folk partially cleaned up for the Big Sunday Occasion. The men were mostly farmers, a few in the catering industry, looking uncomfortable in their clean shirts, jackets and ties. The women, in skirts or dresses and cardigans, all with their heads covered, looked less out of place. Mostly the sexes sat apart on opposite sides of the aisle.

Suddenly everyone stood up and watched as an ecclesiastic procession came up the aisle. In the vanguard were about a dozen small boys, some as young as six, all dressed in long flowing garments topped with a ruff. They wore large heavy crosses, almost down to their navels. They were followed by eight fully-grown men, wearing the adult version of the young choirboys' garments, topped with larger ruffs and larger crosses. After them came two more adult men, probably trainee priests, one carrying a huge cross, which bore the body of Christ. The other carried a chalice. The parish priest brought up the rear.

When the procession reached the altar, the trainee priests swung two huge urns, sending incense as far around the church as possible. Some members of the congregation, including Claire, started coughing. Liam crossed himself again.

The parish priest made a short welcoming speech and the congregation knelt down. He mumbled what Claire imagined were prayers in a language she didn't understand. In fact, all of the service was in a language she didn't understand, which she assumed was Gaelic. The one respite were the hymns, sung in English from a hymn-sheet to tunes that Claire knew well.

About half an hour into the service most members of the congregation, including Liam, went up the aisle, about a dozen at a time, and knelt at the altar. Claire watched, fascinated, as the priest served them a morsel to eat and a drink from a golden chalice. This must be Holy Communion, she thought.

As the service ended, the congregation faced the centre aisle, crossing themselves again as the ecclesiastic procession returned solemnly back the way it had come. The service was over. To Claire it seemed to have lasted all morning. In fact it had only taken forty minutes.

Claire followed Liam to the Church door, where the parish priest shook the hand of each member of the congregation and wished them 'good day.'

As they got into the car Liam asked: 'what did you think of it?'

'Well at least I knew the hymn tunes,' replied Claire, trying to be positive, 'but I didn't understand a word the priest said, which I assume was Gaelic.'

'No, it was Latin. Didn't you learn Latin at school?'

'Yes, of course, but it didn't sound a bit like what we've just heard.'

'Ecclesiastical Latin,' said Liam with a laugh.

Liam switched on the ignition and drove towards Newport, where he had booked a table for lunch at what he presumed was the best hotel. Hopefully it'll be better than the Achill Head Hotel, he thought.

Back at the Achill Head Hotel Claire decided to have a rest. She had found the whole morning strangely unsettling, particularly the Holy Communion. She wondered why Liam never attended Mass in London. Did he attend today because he would shortly be seeing his family for the first time in about five years? Was he doing penance for them?

Liam walked down to Keel Strand, taking the pedestrian shortcut he remembered of old. Keeping his shoes and socks on – too much hassle to remove them – he walked down towards the sea as far as decorum allowed. To his surprise and delight a currach was slowly coming in towards the shore. Arriving in the shallow water, two men jumped out and pulled the boat out of the water onto the sand. Liam decided to pass the time of day. Since their arrival on Achill Island just over a week ago the only locals they had actually spoken to were the scruffy waiter at the Achill Head Hotel and the parish priest at the end of the church service this morning.

As he approached, one of the men looked up. 'Well, bless my soul, if it isn't Liam O'Malley.' He walked up to Liam and gave him a friendly clap on the shoulder. 'Begorrah, Liam, and I thought you was in London, up to great things in high places.'

'Yes, I live in London now with my wife. We've just returned to Achill Island for a holiday.'

'A wife, God bless us! And I didn't know you was married at all, at all.'

'So you haven't seen my family since I left five years ago?'

'No and I haven't at all, at all. And how's London life treating you, Liam? You must miss the sea. Are there any lakes around in London with boats on 'em?'

Liam laughed. 'Oh, yes. There are lakes with boats in London – but nothing like this.' He waved a hand towards the sea.

'And how would you like a boat trip for old time's sake, Liam?'

'I'd love it... but I don't know if my wife... She's not too keen on going out on the water.'

'Can't you leave the wife out of it... just for the once? We're going out tonight around nine o'clock, aren't we, Paddy?'

'Sure an' we are, Brendan. The late evening's the best time for mackerel. Meet us down here at nine o'clock tonight, Liam, if you can.'

'I'll have to explain it all to my wife...' Liam sounded doubtful.

'Let's leave it open,' suggested Brendan. 'If you're here by nine o'clock, you're on. If not, we'll go out on our own as usual.'

'OK. That sounds fine to me.' Liam shook both their hands. 'Bye, now. Hope to see you at nine o'clock tonight.'

Then he made his way back up the beach to the Achill Head Hotel.

Over dinner Liam explained to Claire that he had met two of the fishermen who used to take him out in their boat when he was a boy.

'They've invited us to join them this evening.'

'Us? They've invited me as well?'

'Of course. You're my wife. They'd love to meet you.'

'I'd like to meet them too, Liam. I like meeting anyone connected with your childhood. You know that. But, quite honestly, I don't really want to go out in a boat. I'm a very poor swimmer so I'm not much good on the water.'

'Yes, so you said the other day. Would you mind if I went out on my own? Just with the two fishermen, I mean. They're totally reliable. Nothing will go wrong.'

'Of course you must go. I'm all for reliving one's childhood. What time are you planning to leave?'

'Nine o'clock.'

'So late?'

'Mackerel prefer the dark.'

Claire laughed. 'Unlike me. That's fine, darling. Of course you must go. What time will you be back?'

'Between midnight and one am. I'll creep in without disturbing you.'

'Don't worry. I'll be fast asleep by midnight.'

Liam left Claire in the lounge with a large brandy and made his way down to the beach. Paddy and Brendan greeted Liam warmly and suggested he climb into the boat on dry land. Then they pushed it into the water and jumped in. It was a beautifully calm evening and as they watched the sun setting slowly to the west in front of them, they were all sure they had a wonderful evening ahead.

Claire woke up in the morning at eight o'clock and stretched out towards Liam's side of the bed, but it was empty. He must be in the bathroom, she thought. She went along the corridor and called through the bathroom door: 'Liam, are you there?' But there was no answer. Back in the bedroom she looked at the bedside clock. It was ten minutes past eight. Perhaps Liam was already downstairs having breakfast? She washed, dressed and went downstairs. Their usual table was empty. There was no sign of Liam. The waiter appeared, looking even shabbier than before.

'Morning, m'am. Is sir having a lie in?'

'No. I thought he would be down here.'

Claire ordered breakfast. Perhaps the fishing excursion had lasted all night and Liam would appear at any moment. But she continued her meal alone and in silence. After breakfast she went to the front porch and looked down at the beach. The sand's surface was rough and covered in debris, as if a storm had occurred in the night. A storm? No. Impossible. Not a storm on the one night that Liam had taken a boat trip. She went to the lounge, sat down at the piano and started to play Beethoven's *Pathétique* Sonata. She had just started on the beautifully calm slow movement in A Flat major when there came a knock on the door. She stopped abruptly. 'I'm so sorry to interrupt your beautiful playing, madam. Are you Mrs O'Malley?'

'Yes.'

'I'm the hotel manager. I must ask you to be good enough to step into my office for a moment. The Garda – that is the Police, wish to speak to you.

Claire followed the hotel manager into his office where two policemen were standing, their hands crossed in front of them.

'Good morning, madam,' said the taller officer. 'Please sit down. If you don't mind, I'll get straight to the point. I'm afraid I have some very bad news. There's been a serious accident.'

'Accident?' Claire felt herself go cold. Her heart was thumping loudly and she kept clenching and unclenching her fists.

'I'm afraid so, madam. A storm blew up unexpectedly in the night. The fishermen sent an SOS by torchlight and a rescue crew was sent out. They found the boat – a small currach – but there was no sign of any of the occupants. A full search will be made of course, but there is little hope of finding anyone alive. I'm so sorry, madam and I offer you my deepest condolences.'

Claire gave a piercing scream and fainted.

Chapter Five

When Claire woke up several hours later she didn't know where she was. She was lying on a hard, narrow single bed, half surrounded by a curtain. Propping herself up, she looked around the side of the curtain, where she saw an endless row of similar beds. A female, dressed like Florence Nightingale, appeared at her side.

'How are you, love? Feeling a little better?'

'Where am I? What's happened?'

'You're in hospital.'

'Why?'

'You've had a bad shock.'

'Where's Liam?'

'Your husband?'

'Yes. Where is he?'

The nurse raised her hand and a male figure appeared at the side of the bed. He was dressed in black, wearing the dog collar of a priest.

'Father, she wants to know where her husband is.'

'She doesn't remember anything?'

'It seems not.'

'What's the vicar doing here?' enquired Claire.

'Sure and he isn't the vicar, darlin'. He's the parish priest. He's here to help you remember what happened to your husband.'

VALERIE HANSARD

The priest sat down on the chair by the bed and took Claire's hand. 'Your husband went out in a fishing boat – a small currach – last night to help the fishermen catch mackerel. Unfortunately a storm blew up and the boat capsized. There was no hope for them at all.'

There was complete silence while Claire tried to absorb this terrible information. 'Were the bodies recovered?'

'Not yet, my love. But they'll be found all right.'

'And then there'll be a funeral?'

'Yes.'

Claire rolled over and sobbed her heart out into the hospital pillow.

Claire spent two days in hospital in Galway Town, receiving excellent care. On the third day Liam's sister, Nora came to collect her, bringing with her Claire's suitcase, packed by the management at the Achill Head Hotel. Nora was friendly, although a little aloof. Claire felt that her brother's accident had been an inconvenience rather than a tragedy.

'Couldn't you have stopped Liam going out in that boat?' Nora asked in the car on the way to Westport.

'How could I have stopped him? He just wanted to relive his childhood, the way we all like to sometimes. He was in excellent hands. He'd known both the fishermen since he was a child. It didn't look as if anything could have gone wrong.'

'A storm was forecast,' said Nora. 'The fishermen should have known about it.'

Claire felt there was no answer to that remark, so they continued driving on in silence.

'Have you ever been to Westport before?' asked Nora.

'Yes. Just once. Liam took me to a Catholic Mass and then out to lunch.'

'Do you often go to Mass?'

'No. It was my first time.'

'Why was that?'

'I'm not a Catholic.'

'Oh! But you married one.'

'Yes.'

'Well, this is Westport - your second visit.'

Claire looked out of the side window and saw the sea appearing again. They drove into the town, which was quiet, with very few residents around. The houses were of the early Victorian style and reminded Claire of some of the villages in the south of England. Nora parked the car in front of one of the smaller, shabbier ones.

'Well, here we are. Welcome to Westport.'

Nora ushered Claire into a sitting room with a bay window overlooking an overgrown front garden. 'We call this the parlour. You would probably call it the lounge.'

No, the living room, thought Claire, but said nothing.

'I'll take your luggage up. Would you like to see your room?'

The spare bedroom was on the top floor, small but cheerfully decorated and furnished with a double bed, wardrobe, chest-of-drawers and two bedside tables. Claire sat down on the bed. Well, here I am, she thought, in Liam's sister's house – without Liam. Liam is dead. But his body has yet to be found. She knew she was about to cry.

'Would you like to come down for a cup of tea?' enquired Nora.

'Maybe later. I'll just sit here for a while, if I may.'

When Nora had left the room, Claire turned face downwards on the bed and wept.

The next two weeks were the most stressful of Claire's entire life. She didn't really feel welcomed by Nora and her husband, Seumas and found it extremely difficult to settle into a new household routine. The food and the meal hours were quite different to what she was accustomed to and she had little appetite. Nora served a cooked breakfast promptly at eight am, for which Claire was expected to arrive punctually. She managed this for three days and then suggested that instead of a full meal she could make herself a cup of coffee later in the morning.

'I'm not used to a cooked breakfast,' she explained. Fortunately Nora agreed.

Lunch was served, again promptly at half past twelve, consisting of over-cooked meat and vegetables and a huge mountain of floury potatoes. Claire struggled both with the amount of food and the poor quality of the cooking. High tea, a new term to Claire, was served at a quarter to six, consisting of lunch leftovers – mostly Claire's – bread and jam and, of course, tea. Claire was already missing wine with a good dinner. At half past nine they all gathered again around the kitchen table for cocoa and biscuits, from which she usually excused herself.

There were three children aged eight, ten and twelve, who just said 'hello' when they saw her and then disappeared. But in addition to Liam's tragic death, Claire had no piano to play. A piano would have been a tremendous consolation and have helped to occupy her. So she filled in the time trying to read and taking brief walks in the bleak empty town. The waiting was a torment and lasted for over two weeks.

By the beginning of the second week there was still no news of Liam's whereabouts, so Nora felt duty bound to suggest some distraction.

'Would you like to visit my brother, Donal?' she suggested to Claire at breakfast. 'He lives on a small farm about half an hour's drive from here on the far side of the Croagh Patrick Mountain. It might just help to take your mind off this terrible waiting for news.' She looked anxiously at Claire across the table.

Claire played with her toast. 'I don't mind. Nothing will ease the pain of waiting, but at least it would be something definite to do.'

Nora went out to the post office and sent her brother a telegram. 'Claire distraught awaiting news. Possible lunch with you today?'

An hour later the reply was delivered to her door. 'Come now. Pub lunch.'

I really must get a telephone installed, thought Nora, as she told Claire about the new plan. In a few minutes they were in the car and driving out of Westport along what appeared to Claire was a vast empty space. On the right was the sea; on the left was flat bog-land with a mountain appearing in the distance.

'Clew Bay,' explained Nora.

'And the mountain?'

'Croagh Patrick. Liam and Dermot used to climb it in their teens.'

'Did Donal climb it too?'

'No. He wasn't interested.'

The road, now unsurfaced, narrowed and swung around to the left. They had left Croagh Patrick behind and three small islands appeared far out to sea.

'Inishturk, Inishbofin and Inishark,' said Nora.

'Are they inhabited?'

'No. Not any more. I think the last inhabitants probably died in the potato famine, which began in 1845 and ended in 1849. But many people managed to survive by emigrating to the United States.'

Claire shivered. 'How awful. Ireland has certainly had a very chequered past.'

'I don't think the present is without problems either.'

Nora slowed down and turned into a large neglected-looking farmyard. The car lurched over huge potholes and copious puddles threw filthy water over the windows. At the far end was a dilapidated one-storey stone cottage, several broken tiles lying on the ground beside it. On the right was a vast outhouse, the roof sagging, the windows cracked. As Nora tried in vain to find a dry space in which to park, an unkempt-looking man came out of the cottage. He wore a check shirt with the sleeves rolled up, hanging over baggy trousers with frayed knees. A flat cap sat at an awkward angle on his balding head. He lurched rather than walked in ill-fitting Wellington boots, his feet splayed out, and his shoulders hunched.

Claire felt her stomach tighten. How on earth could Liam have had a brother looking like an unwashed tramp? Will he smell? Horror of horrors: will he cook and serve lunch? Claire couldn't imagine herself being able to eat anything prepared by such a depraved-looking human being. She remained in the car as Nora got out to greet her brother. They exchanged a faint peck on the cheek. Now it's my turn, thought Claire.

Donal opened the front passenger door to reveal a large puddle. Claire hesitated.

'I'll lift ye out,' suggested Donal, and before Claire had time to protest, or even think, she found herself being carried into the cottage and placed on a very shabby armchair.

'There ye' are. It's good to meet ye',' said Donal cheerfully.

'Yes, of course. It's nice to meet you too,' lied Claire.

Donal suggested he would show them around his farm.

'In all those puddles!' Nora sounded rather alarmed.

'I'll get ye's some boots,' suggested Donal.

Kitted out in ill-fitting Wellington boots, Donal escorted the two ladies around his rundown farm. There were two chestnut shire-horses and their carts in the outhouse. As Donal stroked their white blazes, the horses threw up their heads in the air and whinnied, as if in protest. Claire and Nora followed Dolan through puddles, some quite deep, as they made their way behind the shabby cottage to view the land beyond. There were about twenty sheep and perhaps a dozen cows sharing a field, quietly grazing. At least they are out in the fresh air with no danger of a building collapsing on them, thought Claire. After some general comments on the habits, advantages and disadvantages of his flock, Donal looked at his watch.

'It's almost midday. Dinnertime.'

'Here?' asked Claire in some alarm, not daring to correct her brother-in-law's misnomer of lunch.

'Ah, no! Sure I t'ought we'd go to t'e pub. I'm not t'at much of a cook.'

As they piled into Nora's car, Claire was relieved to take off the ill-fitting boots and put on her own comfortable shoes. She wondered if Donal would collect a pair of shoes from the cottage, but he climbed into the back seat still wearing the hunky Wellingtons. He directed Nora to the pub down another narrow unsurfaced road about ten minutes away. Claire sat in silence during the journey, glad to be left in peace. The pub was old but solid looking and the car park was covered in fine gravel. Inside a fire was burning in an old-fashioned grate and there were about a dozen well-scrubbed tables with matching benches. It was empty and silent. Dolan indicated a table next to the fire and went up to the bar.

'Hi t'ere, Colum! It's Dolan. I've brought me family in t'e hopes ye can give us a bite to eat.'

The barman appeared, wiping his hands on a grubby cloth. 'Hi, Dolan!' He came up to the table. 'Nice to meet ye, ladies. And what can I offer ye? Stout or draft beer? Beer's good around here.' He looked directly at Nora.

'I'll have a lemonade.'

'No lemon. Just orange. And you, young lady…?'

Donal was about to introduce Claire as Liam's widow, but thought better of it.

'Any chance of a glass of white wine?' asked Claire.

'White wine!' exclaimed the barman, as if he'd just been asked to fly to the moon. ''Tis not a t'ing t'at's drunk much around t'ese parts. But I'll look into it for ye. Donal, your usual pint of stout?'

'Yes please, Colum.'

'I'll serve t'e drinks what I've got first and t'en have a look for t'e wine,' explained Colum to Claire.

'Yes, of course. That's fine.'

Colum pulled the pint, poured the orangeade and placed the glasses on the table.

'I won't be long,' he said, leaving the pub by a side door. Ten minutes later he was back with a dusty bottle of wine. 'New Zealand. I hope it's okay. I must've had it a while.'

'Thank you for your trouble. I'm sure it'll be lovely.'

Colum pulled the cork, set the bottle down on the bar and looked around for a wine glass, but he couldn't find one. He'd never been asked for wine before. So he selected a pint beer glass from the top shelf, poured in the wine and set the glass in front of Claire.

'And here's good luck to ye.'

Claire took a sip. 'Cheers!' As she had expected, the wine was warm. But she continued sipping and by the end of the meal she had finished the entire bottle.

A week later two policemen arrived at the door. Nora let them in and went upstairs to tell Claire.

'The Garda have arrived and would like to speak to you.'

The policemen were extremely kind. 'We think we've found your husband's body, Mrs O'Malley. Do you think you could accompany us to the mortuary?'

'May I come too?' asked Nora. 'He *was* my brother.'

'Of course, ma'am.' Claire and Nora followed the policemen to their car.

The visit to the mortuary was a nightmare out of all proportion. Three bodies lay on concrete slabs, covered in plastic sheets with just their faces visible. Claire reached for Nora's hand, hoping she wouldn't vomit. As they approached the first body, Claire was riveted with horror. The face was grey and swollen and the head was still covered with hair.

'Yes,' said Claire, 'that's my husband.'

They left without glancing at the other two bodies.

Later a hearse arrived outside the house and the coffin was installed in the front room that Liam's family called the parlour. The lid had been removed so the family could visit him and kneel down beside him to pray. It had taken the Sea Rescue Service over two weeks to recover the three bodies. The coffin would remain in the parlour for two days so that all the neighbours who wished could pay their last respects. This was the usual custom in the West of Ireland. Claire was not consulted. She was treated as if she were an outsider. On the third day after the arrival of the coffin, Nora informed Claire that Liam's funeral would take place the following day in the Church of Saint Mary Magdalene in Westport.

'It will be a Requiem Mass,' explained Nora. 'It always is in our church.'

Claire was given no further information, neither was she allowed any personal input.

On the morning of the funeral Claire alarmed for eight o'clock. Opening the curtains, she saw the rain was pouring down in torrents. Her beloved Liam's burial day. Of course it was bound to rain, especially in this remote part of the world. She had no idea whether Nora would serve one of her inedible cooked breakfasts, but she had no intention of finding out. She washed and inspected her wardrobe. When Liam had planned the Achill Island holiday, Claire had no idea it would end with his funeral, so she hadn't packed a mourner's outfit. But, true to form, she had brought with her some smart evening-wear, including a black skirt and shirt. A dark coat? She would have to ask Nora if she could lend her one.

As arranged, the undertakers arrived promptly at ten o'clock. The six pallbearers carried the coffin out of the front room; the lid already closed, and placed it carefully in the hearse outside the front door. Claire had expected a black limousine to take her and close family members to the church, but instead she was guided into the front passenger seat of one of the family cars. Slowly following the hearse, the journey to the Church of Saint Mary Magdalene took a good twenty minutes. They were followed by at least thirty cars and a long line of policemen guarded the route. Arriving at the church, the coffin was borne in by the pallbearers and placed facing the altar. Claire and close family members followed and sat in the front row. Slowly the other mourners arrived and sat behind. Everyone, except Claire, crossed themselves, and waited in silence for the service to begin.

As the ecclesiastic procession came slowly up the aisle, the congregation crossed themselves again. To Claire it was a familiar scene; reminiscent of the Mass that Liam had taken her to just over two weeks ago. But as this was a Requiem Mass, there were no familiar hymns sung in English from a hymn sheet. As before, the entire service was in Latin, the music consisting only of medieval music, which sounded to Claire as if fourteenth century monks were chanting. The whole service lasted well over an hour. As the ecclesiastic procession wound slowly down the aisle, the mourners followed them to the graveyard, where a large grave had been dug. As the pallbearers lowered the coffin into the hole, the grave-diggers covered it with earth. Liam was now buried deep in the ground. There would be no ashes for Claire to take back with her to London.

The congregation left the graveyard in complete silence. Everyone got into their vehicles and one by one, they drove off. Claire, Nora and Seumas were the first to arrive back at the house, where, to Claire's utter amazement, a bevy of caterers had taken over the entire place. Extra tables and chairs had been brought in and each table was covered with a white linen tablecloth and sparkling cutlery. On the sideboard were several piles of plates and serving dishes piled high with sandwiches, crisps, cakes and biscuits. There were crates of beer and wine stacked on the floor, unopened boxes beside them, presumably containing glasses. Claire was quite mystified by the whole procedure.

'What's going on?' she asked Nora. 'Surely we're not having a party? We've just buried my husband.'

'It's the wakes,' explained Nora, 'an old Irish tradition to hold a party for the dead. To welcome them to heaven, I suppose. Liam will surely be in heaven by now.'

'Am I expected to attend?'

'Expected, yes. I would have thought so. But as a foreigner I'm sure you would be excused if you didn't want to stay.'

So I'm considered a foreigner, thought Claire. But if I don't stay, where shall I go? Upstairs to my room? There's nowhere else. Hunger was beginning to assail her. As she had eaten very little in the last two weeks, she was beginning to feel a severe lack of nourishment. She felt limp and hollow. She sat down on a sofa in the bow window of the front room, called the parlour, hysteria beginning to surface. Slowly the mourners arrived and came up to offer their condolences.

'Your Liam was such a wonderful man...'

'He was so thoughtful...'

'So clever...'

'A terrible tragedy for you to suffer so far away from home...'

'How long will you be staying with us?'

Suddenly everyone, the mourners and the family included, became extremely attentive. Claire was offered endless sandwiches, salads, cakes and biscuits and glass after glass of wine. The wine tasted extremely good, and apart from the bottle in the rough pub a few days ago, she had not drunk any for over two weeks, so it went straight to her head. Then the music started up with a violinist playing traditional Gaelic numbers. To Claire it sounded very strange, not unpleasant but completely foreign. As the music played on, other musicians joined in. There were more violinists, a cellist and a harpist. Some people started to sing and other voices accompanied them. The instrumental group, still playing, made its way slowly to the kitchen at the back of the house and the dancing began. More and more couples joined in, keeping in time to the instrumental group in the background.

Worn out and unable to communicate with anyone or anything, Claire crept quietly up to her bedroom and dropped, exhausted, into bed. Downstairs the wakes continued without the principal mourner until well into the small hours.

Two days later Claire approached Nora with considerable apprehension.

'My flight for London leaves at midday tomorrow from Shannon Airport. Is there a train I can catch?'

'A train! No, not in this part of Ireland.'

'How do I get there? Can I hire a car?'

'No, no. Don't worry. I'll drive you down. Are you sure you want to leave so soon?'

'Well, I have a job to go to. A new term starts in a few weeks at the school where I teach music, so I have to do some preparation.'

Although the flat was deathly quiet, Claire was enormously relieved to be home. The tragedy of Liam's death hadn't fully sunk in and now she had the onerous task of informing relatives and friends of the terrible accident. She unpacked, poured herself a glass of wine and ordered a Chinese take-away. Tomorrow's burdens could wait.

She realised that after such an appalling tragedy, it would be a great effort to return to teaching. Fortunately, she had over a month before term started. A month to try and organise her fraught emotions and apply herself to some serious piano practice. During the lunch hour on the first day of term she went to see the headmistress to inform her of Liam's death. The head was extremely sympathetic and said if there was anything she could do to help, would Claire please let her know. Claire had also received tremendous sympathy from friends, but of course now she was entirely on her own. And everyone else knew that too.

A week later she received a letter from Nora requesting payment for the funeral. In an itemised list with all the figures opposite, every expense was detailed down to the last penny. All the food and drink consumed at the wakes was included. The total came to almost three hundred pounds. In complete shock, Claire sat down heavily on the sofa. She read though the list again, barely understanding the figures. Then she got up, walked over to the bin, tore both sheets to shreds and threw them away.

A month later she missed her period. Just stress, she thought. But when she missed the second one she went to see her doctor, who took a pregnancy test. Three days later she received a letter in the post informing her that she was pregnant. Next year, around the beginning of April she would give birth to Liam's baby – without Liam. Liam would never know about his baby. She would have to bring up the child entirely on her own. How would she manage financially apart from anything else? She would have to give up her teaching job in order to devote time to the baby. Although Liam always said he would like a family, Claire wanted to develop her career as a professional pianist. But not now. She couldn't imagine being able to practise the piano with a baby howling in its cot. What about an abortion? It was strictly illegal, of course, even in Protestant Britain. But there were underground, back street abortionists. She would have to give the whole matter very careful consideration.

Claire called her friend, Lucy.

'Claire! That's wonderful news!'

'Wonderful? I think it's ghastly news. I'm a widow now. How am I going to be able to bring up a baby all on my own?'

'You'll have help, surely. I'll help when I can.'

'Thank you, Lucy. I'm sure you will. But it's the "when I can" that's the operative phrase.'

'Yes, I understand. But there are always the social services. Have you discussed it with your GP?'

'Not in great detail. Of course he knows I'm a widow, but I haven't told him about the piano. I can't give that up. It's all I've ever wanted to do: to be a professional pianist.'

'Yes. I realise that. What about your mother? Would she help? How old is she?'

'She'll be fifty when the baby is born.'

'She sounds the perfect age. And your Dad died a few years ago?'

'Yes. Five years ago.'

'Are you close to your mother?'

'Less close than I was since my marriage to Liam. She was horrified when I married a Roman Catholic.'

'Any sisters?'

'No sisters. Just two older brothers who emigrated as soon as they could. Chris lives in Auckland, New Zealand and Simon lives in Toronto.'

'Do you hear from them? Any letters?'

'No. Not very often.'

'It looks as if the main help will have to come from your mother.'

'Yes. Unfortunately.'

Claire stood sideways in front of the bedroom mirror and stroked her stomach. Yes. The bump was beginning to show. At five months pregnant it would, of course. She really ought to tell her mother before any awkward questions were asked. That meant a tedious trip out to Hemel Hempstead. What a pain. She had been so relieved when her parents had allowed her to move into 'digs' near the Marylebone Road when she had won her scholarship to the Royal Academy of Music in 1948. And that was only six years ago. Such a lot had happened in her life since then. She must call her mother to arrange a time and a date.

Gwen Tebbit was slim and petite. She dressed with care and had her hair tinted regularly. Clive's prostate cancer diagnosis had come as a huge shock; his death one year later had been an even greater one. Although there had been a sixteen-year age gap between them, she hadn't expected to be widowed at the age of only forty-four. Still, there were other men around, some younger than she was, some older. She hoped Claire was also looking around. Aged only twenty-five she really shouldn't continue living on her own. To Gwen, Liam's death by drowning was totally inexplicable. Why would anyone want to take a small boat out on the Atlantic Ocean after dark? Claire would be here to lunch tomorrow. Gwen felt her daughter's visit was rather overdue. But Gwen usually expected more of other people than she was prepared to offer herself.

Claire selected a loose-fitting dress with a long skirt, fashionable at the time. She wasn't sure if she could face telling her mother about the forthcoming birth. She and Liam had only been married for three years before his tragic death. Anyway, whatever she said her mother would make her opinions quite clear. She always did.

'You do look pretty in that dress, dear.'

'Thank you, Mummy.'

Gwen bustled about with plates and serving dishes. The carving knife and fork were poised above a well-browned roast chicken. 'Leg or breast?'

'Oh, leg, please.' Claire held out her plate and then helped herself to green beans and potatoes. 'This looks delicious.'

'And how is the teaching going?' enquired Gwen.

'Oh, fine, thank you, Mummy. I'm enjoying it. Above all I need the money now that Liam's gone.'

'Of course. We all need money, especially us widows.'

The lifeless conversation drifted around for a couple of hours. At half past two Claire glanced at her watch. 'Mummy, I must leave you now. It'll take me a good hour to get home and I need to do another two hours' piano practice.'

Gwen stood up and showed her daughter to the front door. 'So, you're still practising the piano?'

'Yes, Mummy. I've always wanted to be a professional pianist.'

'Oh, I see.' Gwen sounded surprised. 'I thought you had given up that idea once you applied for the teaching post.'

Claire sighed quietly. 'No, Mummy. To perform in public has always been my main aim in life.'

As Claire was preparing a light evening meal, the phone rang.

'Claire? It's Lucy. How did the lunch go with your mother? Did you tell her about the baby?'

'No. I didn't. The right moment didn't seem to crop up.'

'I see. Well, you'll have to tell her soon.'

'Yes. I know.'

The rehearsal for the piano trio recital was going well. This time the venue would be the Fairfield Hall in Croyden, in south London. Next time they were all hoping for the Wigmore Hall in London's West End. Claire directed the rehearsal with her usual aplomb and expertise. Sarah, the violinist and Charles, the cellist were the other performers. At the end of the rehearsal there was the usual round of self-congratulation. As she tidied away her music, Claire let a sheet fall on the floor. Charles was beside her in no time.

'Please allow me, Claire. Expectant mothers shouldn't bend over.'

Claire was surprised. 'So you noticed?'

'Yes, of course. We both have. It's not something that can be kept a secret indefinitely. When is it due?'

'The beginning of April.'

'Just before the concert then.'

'Yes.'

'Who's going to look after it before the next concert?'

'I've got to work that out.'

'Aaah.'

Claire went to see her headmistress. 'Miss Haywood, I'm expecting a baby at the beginning of April.'

'Congratulations!'

'Thank you. But I'm not sure that's appropriate now that I'm widowed.'

'I see your point. Have you made arrangements?'

'For after the baby's birth?'

Miss Haywood nodded.

'Probably not sufficient arrangements. Would it be possible for you to engage a temporary replacement until...'

'I'm sure we can find a supply teacher for a few months, Claire.'

'Thank you, Miss Haywood.'

Gwen was standing on the doorstep when Claire arrived at the house in Hemel Hempstead. Claire was now finding walking a challenge and she couldn't bend down at all. Gwen noticed her daughter's condition right away.

'Claire! There's a baby on the way and you never told me!'

'That's why I'm here. To tell you in person.'

Gwen led the way into the house and indicated the sofa. 'I hope it's Liam's baby.'

'Of course it's Liam's baby!' Claire was horrified. 'Who else's baby would it be?'

'Well, I don't know. The young get up to all sorts of nefarious activities nowadays.'

A large part of Claire wanted to leave right away, but she was hungry and knew she wouldn't be able to face the journey home without some kind of sustenance.

'When is it due?'

'The beginning of April.'

'Who will look after it?'

'Well, I suppose I will…with a little help…'

'From me?'

'Thank you, Mummy.'

The concert at the Fairfield Hall received rave reviews. *The recital began with Mozart's Piano Trio in C major K 548, followed by Beethoven's Piano Trio Opus 1 No 1, and ended, to tumultuous applause, with the Brahms Violin and Piano Sonata in A major Opus 100.'*

The baby was two weeks late.

'Many first babies are overdue,' explained Claire's GP, rather as if she should have known it herself. Then the waiting became an agony. It reminded Claire of the appalling two weeks she was forced to wait for the recovery of Liam's body after the terrible fishing tragedy. Finally, when her waters broke she called an ambulance to take her to UCH. Her labour lasted twenty-two hours, ending with a forceps delivery under a general anaesthetic. When she woke up a nurse in a dark blue uniform placed a small bundle in her arms.

'Congratulations. It's a boy. I hope that's what you wanted.'

I didn't want a baby at all, thought Claire. But she said nothing.

In 1955 most new mothers spent a week in hospital. Due to her forceps delivery, considered at that time to be a minor operation, Claire spent almost two weeks on the maternity ward. This left her some time to work out how she was going to cope with her new life.

Chapter Six

When Claire's baby was finally born on 21 April 1955, Gwen was her first visitor.

'Hello, darling. How are you feeling?'

'Tired. But I'm OK.'

Gwen looked at the baby lying in his hospital cot beside her daughter's bed. The sister on duty had told her that her grandchild was a boy.

'Are you pleased you've had a boy?'

'I'm not pleased I've had a baby. The timing is quite inappropriate.'

'Births are often badly timed. You'll get used to it.'

'I suppose I'll have to.'

'Has your milk come in yet?'

'Well, my breasts are huge and beginning to dribble, so I suppose it's on its way.'

'Are the nurses being helpful?'

'Yes. When they've got time. There are nine other newborn babies on the ward.'

'Has he got a name?'

'I'm thinking of Liam James.'

'To be called Liam or James?'

'Probably James.'

'That sounds good,' said Gwen with some relief. 'At least it's an English name.'

'There's nothing wrong with Irish names.'

'No, of course not. But an English name is easier to handle in England. Will he be baptised a Roman Catholic?'

'Mummy, I haven't got that far yet. I haven't even filled in his birth certificate.'

Gwen leant over and gave Claire a light peck on the cheek. 'I'll come in again tomorrow.'

Claire smiled faintly up at her mother. 'Thank you, Mummy. That would be lovely.'

At the arranged discharge time Gwen collected Claire from hospital and drove her and baby James out to Hemel Hempstead. It was what Claire expected and what she had been dreading. But she couldn't see there was any alternative. How could she, a widow, look after a newborn baby on her own? It wasn't just that she was on her own. She knew nothing whatsoever about newborn babies, and nothing about bringing up children. She didn't think Liam had known much about bringing up children either, but at least there would have been two of them doing it together. And she was sure that Liam would have learnt quickly how to attend to his son's needs. But Liam was dead and buried far away in Westport, County Mayo, in the most westerly and barren part of Ireland. He had come to live and study in London to escape the remoteness of his own country, but he had failed in his escape. He could never return now to civilisation. All that remained of him and had returned to London was his seed in Claire's uterus. In the nine months after Liam's death his seed had developed into his and Claire's baby. The baby now lay in a cot on the back seat of his grandmother's car, on his way to live in Hemel Hempstead. He was a fatherless baby with a bleak future. And instead of being reared, as most babies are, by both his parents, he would be brought up by two widows, who had very few values in common.

It was the nights that Claire dreaded the most. During the day James slept most of the time, just waking when Claire picked him up to feed him. Her natural instinct was to let him sleep until he woke up hungry. But Gwen was having none of that.

'You must feed him on a regular basis, Claire. Four hourly feeds are the norm.'

'Why can't I just feed him when he wakes up in his own good time?' objected Claire. 'Babies have no idea what time it is.'

'Regular four hour feeding will develop his sense of time,' insisted Gwen firmly.

As she was woken night after night at two or three am, Claire couldn't see how the four hour daily feeds were developing James's sense of time. At night Gwen slept wearing earplugs, her bedroom door firmly shut. She had no intention of taking part in her grandson's nocturnal life.

Claire struggled with life in Hemel Hempstead for six weeks. During the day her mother interfered with almost every minute detail, as Claire struggled to care for baby James. Gwen watched her daughter breastfeed, complaining that she held the baby at the wrong angle.

'He should be more upright,' she remarked. 'If you hold him too flat he's more likely to have indigestion.'

Claire said nothing. She just thought: why don't you do it? And then: I wonder how you held my brothers and me?

Gwen watched the nappy-changing routine with intense concentration. 'You should always start cleaning at the front. Wipe his little willy first.'

Why can't you call it a penis? thought Claire.

But Claire's greatest problem was that she had no piano. She longed to return to her chamber music but there was no way she could play with other professionals unless she practised for three or four hours a day. But her piano was twenty-five miles away in London. It was too far to take James and too long a time to leave him in Hemel Hempstead in charge of his grandmother. There was only one solution. She had to move back to London. She tried to explain it gently to Gwen.

'Mummy, I have to practice the piano regularly if I'm going to get on with my professional career. I must return to London and my piano.'

'But you've got a new career,' objected Gwen. 'You're a full-time mother.'

'I don't want to be a full-time mother. I want to be a professional pianist.'

'What will happen to James?'

'He'll be fine. Lucy said she would help when she can. There are social services and day care centres.'

'James won't like being in a day care centre.'

'How do you know? He's too young to notice the difference between my care and that of a professional. He'll probably prefer the professional. At least they know what they're doing.'

Claire picked up baby James and went upstairs to pack.

Back in London, with no one to help her care for James, Claire felt under constant pressure. The disrupted nights continued and the days were not that much better. As soon as Claire sat down at the piano, James cried. When she picked him up he stopped crying. She tried leaving him, hoping her playing would soothe him, but to no avail. The louder she played, the louder he cried. She tried putting him over her shoulder to do a bit of one-handed practice on technical exercises, but he didn't like that either.

Then there was the question of money. As Claire was no longer earning, her bank balance was steadily decreasing. It was now mid-June and next week school would restart after the half term break. She called her headmistress at St Paul's School for Girls to ask if there was any chance she could return for the remainder of the summer term, even on a part-time basis.

'I'm really sorry, Claire,' came the reply. 'We agreed that you would return in September. I can't sack your temporary replacement.'

Claire went to see her bank manager. He was more understanding than she had expected and agreed to give her a six month interest free loan. He was shocked by Liam's death.

'As a barrister your late husband had huge earning potential. His death is an appalling tragedy. I'll do what I can to help you.'

Finally, Claire called Charles, the cellist in the piano trio. Charles was sympathetic but not very positive. He enquired how Claire and the baby were doing and how Claire was managing.

'I'm fine. The baby is growing bigger every day but he howls whenever I play the piano. I'll have to work something out so I can return to take part in our concerts. When is the next one?'

'July the twelfth. But Sarah and I have engaged a second violin and a viola. We're planning to become a string quartet.'

A string quartet, thought Claire. Well, that excludes me.

For the moment all life's doors appeared closed. But the piano practice had to continue. Of that Claire was quite adamant.

In mid-July Claire took James to the baby clinic at her doctor's surgery for his three month check up. She was extremely relieved to be told by the sister on duty that James had passed all his tests with flying colours.

'I'll give you both an A star. I suggest you continue breast-feeding for another three months if possible. Even if it's only once a day.'

Claire decided to come straight to the point. 'Of course I'm pleased that everything is going so well. But I really need to get back to work as soon as possible. Is there anywhere I could leave James in care of someone else for about four hours a day?'

'Of course. There's a babies' nursery here. You can leave him as long as you wish. But it's not free. It's seventeen and sixpence an hour.'

Claire knew this was beyond her means until she started earning again. 'I'm not sure I can manage that until I go back to work.'

'What's your job, love?'

'I'm a pianist. I play in public but I need time to practise.'

'Oh, I see,' said the sister, although clearly she didn't.

'I'll have to think about it.'

'Of course.'

On her way out of the surgery Claire saw a notice pinned to the back of the door: 'Receptionist required. Please apply at the desk.'

Claire returned to the reception desk and asked for an application form. She filled it in there and then, went home... and waited.

Being a receptionist in a doctor's surgery was quite a new experience for Claire. Fortunately she had learnt to type at school, and although her skills were now rather rusty, she felt they would return with practice. She was, after all, a professional pianist so her fingers worked better than most other peoples'. She had to be at the reception desk at eight am when the surgery opened. But before that James had to be fed and left in the nursery, so Claire was up at seven. It was an early start but she soon became accustomed to it. There were two younger receptionists, Mavis and Sharon, in their early twenties and Jean, a much older lady in her late fifties. Jean, strict and controlling, was in charge. But she did have a softer side, allowing Claire to slip off about every hour or so to visit James briefly in the nursery.

James thrived in the nursery. By the end of August, aged just over four months, he was gurgling and rolling around on the soft mat placed on the floor. Often he rolled up to another baby, tapping them on the leg or the stomach as if to say: 'please play with me.'

By mid-September Claire returned to her teaching post. The headmistress had generously allowed her to rearrange her teaching hours to maximize James's time in the nursery. Claire had thought through her timetable with great care. Although she urgently needed the money – and fortunately her teaching job paid out far more handsomely than that of surgery receptionist – her top priority was to practice the piano for a minimum of four hours a day. As she was freshest in the morning, she left James in the nursery at eight am and practiced for a good three hours. By now, much to her relief, her milk had dried up and it seemed far easier to bottle-feed James than mess around with milk-soiled clothes. She collected him before midday, gave him another bottle, popped him back in the nursery and was in her school music room by one o'clock. Usually she had finished teaching by four pm, when she collected James and took him home for the rest of the day. By now she was beginning to find her little son quite appealing, so she cuddled him and played with him until he was ready for another spell in his cot. Then she spent another hour or two at the piano. This continued until Christmas, by which time James was eight months old and already beginning to sit up.

Claire was now feeling extremely relieved that she was managing both baby care and her piano practice rather well. But her end goal still eluded her. Since James's birth she hadn't played once in public. She knew she was ready, but she didn't have any engagements. There were two options. One was to play in a chamber group that included the piano. Many of the greatest composers had written outstanding works for piano and violin, piano trios and quartets and many combinations with piano, strings and woodwind. It was just a question of finding the right professional group to play with. She often considered calling Charles to ask if his newly found string quartet could occasionally require her services as a pianist. But something stopped her. Probably pride.

Her other option was to become a soloist. She already had an extensive repertoire of solo works including most of the Mozart, Haydn, Beethoven and Schubert piano sonatas. She also enjoyed playing Chopin's piano sonatas and his shorter works such as the nocturnes, preludes and waltzes. But being a soloist was in quite a different league from that of a chamber music performer. The biggest hurdle was that she would be entirely on her own. She would travel to the venues on her own, stay in obscure hotels on her own and then appear on the platform, completely on her own. The mantle of soloist might be too heavy to bear and could not be undertaken lightly.

Strangely enough, there were very few people with whom Claire could discuss this complicated problem. She visited her mother for Sunday lunch every four or five weeks, taking James along too. Gwen was ecstatic about James's progress, although she continued in her inimitable way to give her own brand of advice. Claire let her mother's extortions go in one ear and out the other, never making any comments. She chatted about her teaching job, mentioning some of her most outstanding students. She said she was eventually planning to return to her performing career but didn't state any specific date. This time Gwen, knowing nothing whatsoever about performing anything in public, said nothing.

Claire met up with Lucy and a few other girl friends, usually for lunch, but sheered away from discussing her life as a professional pianist. The only people with whom she could discuss her performing career were Charles and Sarah, but for the moment she held her peace.

During the school holidays Claire continued to drop James off at the nursery when the time suited her. Now that his place was secured, the hours were quite flexible. This gave her time to go to chamber music concerts and hear other professional musicians perform. She went backstage during the interval to offer her congratulations, in the hope that perhaps she would be invited to join an after-concert party. Her favourite concert hall was the Wigmore Hall in Central London, a venue that topped the list for one of her own performances.

She also attended some chamber music concerts and solo recitals at the Royal Academy of Music, where she had spent three years as a student. But that was almost eight years ago and Claire felt rather daunted by the very young appearance of the present students. She couldn't imagine any professional doors opening in that direction, so she stuck to the Wigmore Hall.

One Monday at lunchtime, she went to a concert for woodwind and strings, being recorded for the BBC Third Programme. Barely an hour long, the programme consisted of Mozart's Oboe Quartet in F major K 370 and the Clarinet Quintet K 581. It was a stunning recital, so Claire decided to go backstage and offer her congratulations. Too bad there's no piano, she thought. But perhaps there is a larger ensemble including a piano. The oboe player was particularly welcoming and thanked her effusively for coming backstage. Chatting over drinks and nibbles he introduced himself as Daniel Braithwaite, explaining that he was the principal oboe in the London Symphony Orchestra and playing chamber music was just a sideline. During Daniel's descriptions of long-haul travel with the LSO, Claire prepared herself for questions about her own career. She couldn't decide how much she should reveal to this extremely attractive oboist, tall, dark and slim with deep-set blue eyes and a slightly receding hairline. In the end all she told him was that she taught the piano at St Paul's School for Girls. She didn't mention her longing to return to the professional musical scene. Nor did she mention being a widow with a baby. She was pleased when Daniel suggested they should exchange phone numbers.

On her first date with Daniel, Claire knew she would have to tell him something about her past life. He was horrified to hear of Liam's death by drowning.

'That's appalling! Was there nothing the boatmen could do to save themselves? I mean, they went out fishing regularly, didn't they? Perhaps they should have listened to the shipping forecast.'

'With hindsight maybe they should have. But I understood they were quite simple people. Fishing was all they did. Achill Island is a pretty backward place. Even Liam thought it was. Third World was one of his expressions.'

'And what did you think of it?'

'I thought it was Third World. The hotel we stayed at was very shabby and out of date.'

'Why did Liam suggest staying there?'

'To revisit his childhood, I suppose.'

'And the family?'

'Very behind the times. They didn't even have a telephone.'

'No telephone in 1954! That's really backward. How did they contact people?'

'They used the public phone box – or sent a telegram.'

'Good God! No wonder Liam wanted to leave Ireland.'

'Yes. But sadly, he's back there now, buried deep in the ground in County Mayo. I didn't even have his ashes to take home with me.'

Daniel took her hand. 'I can't say how sorry – and appalled I am.'

'And what about you, Daniel? How come a handsome man like you isn't married?'

Daniel's story, although quite different from Claire's, was also sad. Four years ago he had become engaged to a violinist, Alice Mildmay, who had high hopes of becoming a soloist. In those days sexual equality was virtually non-existent in the music profession and women were excluded from many of the top orchestras, including the London Symphony Orchestra. As well as being banned from many of the prestigious groups of musicians, women also found it difficult to become solo performers. Ending up in bed with the one or more of the top promoters was par for the course. Which is exactly what Alice Mildmay did. Unfortunately for her relationship with Daniel, Alice became pregnant. Insisting that the baby was Daniel's and the pregnancy would only enrich their relationship, Alice desperately tried to persuade Daniel into an early marriage. But discovering his fiancée's misdemeanour, Daniel knew the dates were wrong. The baby was conceived while he was away in the Far East with the LSO. He broke off the engagement and over a year later he heard that the baby had been born prematurely and had died aged only a few weeks old.

Having exchanged their heart-rending stories, Claire avoided mentioning that she was the mother of an eighteen month old son. Daniel discovered James's existence by accident. Claire had mentioned it was her birthday in a few days time and Daniel had called round to surprise her with a large bunch of flowers. Claire had forgotten she had given Daniel her address as well as her phone number and went to answer the front door, thinking it was a neighbour, who perhaps wanted to borrow something. When she opened the door, there stood Daniel. Beside Claire was James, clutching her leg.

'Oh!' exclaimed Daniel. 'You're baby-sitting.'

'No,' said Claire. 'This is my son, James. I think you'd better come in and then I can explain.'

Daniel and James bonded so well that three months later Daniel moved into Claire's apartment. Daniel had always longed for a son. Claire had always hoped for someone, preferably male, to help her care for Daniel. The new arrangement suited both of them perfectly.

Chapter Seven

In the mid-1950s and well into the 1960s it was unusual for women with children to go out to work. As James wasn't aware of what other people termed 'normal upbringing', he just accepted the fact that his mother worked. When Claire was out, either Daniel or Gwen, James's Granny took care of him. Once he had turned five and started primary school, Granny took care of him during the weekends if both his parents were away. During the week in term time, Claire and Daniel tried to arrange their working hours so that one of them was free to look after James. But this wasn't always possible. As the principal oboist in the London Symphony Orchestra, Daniel travelled abroad a great deal. If both parents were working during the week, Gwen moved in to their London home to look after James.

During his first year at primary school James's friends began to remark that it was not always Mummy who brought and collected him from school.

'Mummy works,' explained James.

'She *works!*' Why? Doesn't your Dad have a job?'

'Yes, of course he does. But Mummy likes working.'

'What does she do?'

'She's a professional pianist.'

'What's that?'

'She plays the piano in public with other musicians and gets paid for it. She teaches the piano too – at St Paul's School for Girls.'

'And what does your Dad do?'

'He plays the oboe in a big symphony orchestra.'

'How strange. Do they play together in public?'

'I don't think so.'

As he grew older James increasingly realised that his life was rather unusual. It was rare that both his parents were at home together in the evening, so they hardly ever ate together. Then, when one or both of his parents were at home, there was the sound of music always being played. To James it seemed like constant noise. Whoever was playing, the music was forever being repeated. One day James asked his mother why they both played so much at home.

'It's called practising,' explained Claire. 'We can't play to the public if we don't get all the notes right beforehand. We wouldn't be paid.'

'Oh, I see,' said James, although he didn't see at all.

James enjoyed school and did well academically. He also excelled on the sports field, particularly at football. And although most of his friends found his home life rather strange, he was invited to their houses for tea after school, or to spend a day in the holidays. But he was rarely allowed to return the invitations.

'Your Dad and I can't really manage with extra young boys here,' Claire tried to explain. 'As you know, we both work.'

'But none of my friends would be in the way,' objected James. 'We could get our own tea and go upstairs to play in my bedroom.'

But his friends were hardly ever allowed to visit. There was always some excuse.

'Are you ready, James?' Daniel called up the stairs.

'Yes. I'm coming, Dad. Just looking for my tie...'

Daniel looked at his watch. 'It's your first day. You mustn't be late...'

'I know – I know...'

James stood at the top of the stairs and looked down at Daniel. 'My last jump?' he suggested.

'Yes, why not. Last jump for your first day in the juniors.'

'Catch!' James threw down his school satchel, which Daniel caught, with evident practise.

'Now me!' James sailed through the air. Daniel staggered back a little as he caught him.

'You're getting heavy. Growing up too fast.' He set the boy down gently and put his arm around him as they went out the front door.

It was Claire who collected James from school. James was a little surprised, as he was expecting Daniel.

'Where's Dad?' he enquired, without even saying hello to his mother.

'At an afternoon rehearsal for tonight's concert.'

'Oh! He never told me.'

'Maybe he forgot.'

'Forgot to tell me – or the rehearsal?'

'James, I don't know – and I don't see that it's important. What's far more important is that you tell me all about your first day of the new term.'

'Well, Sir is far more strict that Miss Hipple was.'

'Sir? You've got a male class teacher. That's good.'

'Why is that good?'

'It's good for boys of your age to have a male teacher.'

'Why?'

'So you get used to men, I suppose.'

'I am used to men. I've got Dad.'

'Yes. I know.' Claire gave her son a light hug. 'Have all the children from the infants gone up to the juniors?'

'Not all. Some of them, mostly boys, have gone on to prep school. What's prep school, Mum? Why is it different from junior school?'

Claire wasn't sure how to answer such a direct question. My goodness, James was growing up fast. 'Well, a prep school is a private school...'

'What does that mean?'

'It means the parents have to pay for it.'

'Do they pay a lot?'

'That depends on the school.'

'Are private schools better than state schools?'

'Again, it depends on the school.'

'So you're Claire Tebbit, Daniel Braithwaite's partner? And you're a professional pianist with some experience. I'm Paul Goodall. I'm the first violin in the Felix quartet. We play a great deal of string quartets of course, but we like to spread our wings a little into piano trios and piano quartets. And then of course there's Mendelssohn's wonderful octet for two string quartets...'

As they shook hands Claire wondered what was coming next.

'Have you ever played at the Wigmore Hall?'

'Just once,' Claire lied. Better to start at the top, she thought. 'I've given several chamber music concerts at the Fairfield Hall in Croyden and in the Harrogate Town

Hall. I've also given two solo recitals in Woodford Green, Essex.'

'Come and play to me,' Paul suggested.

Claire had brought plenty of music with her but she thought it better to perform from memory, despite the fact that as a chamber music pianist she would always have the music in front of her. As Claire walked towards the piano she was relieved to see it was a Steinway. She sat down, adjusted the stool and launched into Beethoven's *Appassionata Sonata* Opus 57. Paul sat in silence, deeply engrossed. When Claire had finished he clapped.

'Excellent! Well done! Beautiful playing. Do you know any of the violin and piano sonatas?'

'Oh, yes. Most of the Mozart, Beethoven and Brahms... and the César Franck, but I haven't played that recently.'

'Let's go for Beethoven's *Spring Sonata*,' suggested Paul. 'It's one of my favourites.'

Musically Claire and Paul bonded well. As the last notes of the *Spring Sonata* died away Paul laid down his violin. 'I think it's time for coffee and a chat.'

The chance meeting with Paul Goodall gave Claire's professional career a tremendous lift. As the core group was a string quartet, Claire wasn't included in all the concerts. But when she did perform with them the reviews were so outstanding that Paul included her in almost every concert, even if it was just for one work.

'*It was the pianist, Claire Tebbit, who supplied the musical inspiration,*' ran *The Times*. And in *The Guardian*: '*Claire Tebbit gave outstanding professional insight into César Franck's Sonata for violin and piano.*'

Claire still taught the piano at St Paul's School for Girls, so her work schedule was very heavy. As the principle oboe in the London Symphony Orchestra, Daniel's performing work had also increased. By then the LSO was considered one of the world's leading symphony orchestras so Daniel travelled abroad a great deal. One week he was in Singapore, the next week Chicago, followed by a three-week series in continental Europe.

By this time James was thirteen years old and about to start in the third year of his comprehensive school.

Claire was delighted – and relieved – that Gwen had remarried. Tony was plain, rather dull, but pleasant; and he seemed to be able to handle being organised by Gwen, which meant that Claire was now free of her mother's control, or most of it. But there were still awkward questions, most of which concerned James.

'I haven't seen James recently, Claire. You hardly ever bring him out here to lunch.'

'Yes, I know, Mummy. I'm really sorry. But James is thirteen now. He's very busy with his social life and all his school work. He goes into the third year of his comprehensive school in September.'

'I know, but I still think he owes something to his Granny. After all, I helped a great deal with his upbringing when he was little so that you could further your career. I spent months living in your house.'

'Yes, Mummy. And I'm most grateful for all your past help. I'll see what I can do next time.'

But what Gwen didn't know was that James didn't know that Daniel was not his father.

'Claire, I think perhaps James should go to boarding school.'

'*Boarding school!* But why?'

'Neither of us has sufficient time to supervise him. After school and in the holidays he's left far too much to his own devices. And because we are both so often out at work, he is rarely able to invite friends here.'

'But he visits them,' Claire objected. 'He enjoys that – especially as he's an only child. And Mother would invite him more often if I suggested it.'

'Yes, I'm sure she would. But she's got Tony to take care of. Or perhaps Tony takes care of her,' remarked Daniel with a twinkle.'

'Perhaps.'

'Although time may be running out I think we should look at some private boarding schools. Some of them take boys rising thirteen. Which brings me to the other question: James must be told that Liam was his father. He's got to know his surname is O'Malley, not Braithwaite. One day, maybe quite soon, he'll need a passport and we'll have to produce his birth certificate.'

'Will you tell him, Dan?'

'OK, if you'd prefer me to.'

'I really would. It's going to be very hard for him.'

James poked about in one of the bottom, rarely opened kitchen drawers. He was looking for something to scrape the filth off his football boots, now lying on a newspaper on the working top. Both his parents were out. His father was away in Cleveland Ohio, playing with the LSO. His mother was rehearsing for another chamber music concert. Always this music, thought James. They care for music more than they care for me. He used to like classical music, especially Bach and Mozart. He had learnt the violin for three years and was considered quite promising. But he had recently given it up. It seemed that classical music was consuming both his parents' lives and he had no wish to be consumed in a similar manner. He couldn't find what he wanted, so he began to empty the drawer and piled the contents onto the worktop. God, these drawers are a mess, he thought. Naturally tidy, he resented the fact that his mother increasingly neglected the housework. As the pile grew higher and he had almost reached the bottom of the drawer, he picked out two documents. He was about to add them to the heap of contents on the worktop when something caught his eye. One was a small green book with a harp embossed in gold in the centre. In the top right hand corner there were three words, each under the other: *Eire - Ireland – Irelande* in gold lettering. In the bottom left hand corner there were three other words in similar gold lettering: *Pas – Passport – Passeport*.

He sat down on a chair, opened it and began to read. On the first page, underneath an official number beginning with E was a name: *Liam James O'Malley, Citizen of Ireland*. On the next page was handwritten: *Born 12 April 1928, Westport, County Mayo, Republic of Ireland. Height 6ft 2 ins. Eyes brown*. On the opposite page was a photo of a young man in his twenties. A sob mounted in James's throat and his breath came in short gasps. He laid the passport down on the kitchen table and picked up the other document, a thin sheet of foolscap paper. Opening it, he realised straight away that it was a death certificate. *Liam James O'Malley: death by drowning 9 July 1954: Achill Island, County Mayo, The Republic of Ireland*.

'This is my Dad!' he shouted. 'I've been cheated! My mother and Daniel have lied to me! My surname's not Braithwaite – it's O'Malley! Daniel's not my Dad. My Dad is dead!'

For a moment he couldn't think straight. He couldn't feel anything. For the last thirteen years, in fact the whole of his life, he had been lied to by his mother and the man he had always known as his father. I've got to get out of here, he thought. It doesn't matter if I'm missed. I'll go to Steven's house. Hopefully he'll be at home. He took his coat off the hallstand, and stuffing the two documents into a pocket, he grabbed a key from behind the door and ran half the way to his friend's house.

Claire laid her music case down on the hall settle and called out: 'hello James! I'm back!' She walked into the living room expecting to see her son curled up on the sofa reading a book. But the room was empty. She went down the two steps to the dining-kitchen at the back of the house, but James wasn't there either. Then she noticed a huge pile of odd assortments, a mixture of rubbish and discarded items all piled up on the working top. Beside the heap was a pair of muddy football boots. James had probably been looking for something to clean his boots. Perhaps he's gone out to visit a friend, she thought. It must be very lonely for him during the holidays with both parents constantly working. Maybe boarding school really *is* the answer. Both parents. It had now become ingrained that Daniel was his real father. Would there be any point in telling James now that this simply isn't true? That his real father had drowned fourteen years ago off an island in the remotest part of Ireland? Claire realises it's on her conscience.

She filled the kettle and plugged it in. Before making her cuppa she thought she should pop upstairs and see if James was in his bedroom. Perhaps he was asleep, tired out by his football match. She knocked softly on the bedroom door, but there was no answer. She opened the door quietly, but the room was empty.

She had barely reached the bottom of the stairs when the phone rang in the living room. Perhaps it was James calling from a friend's house. She picked up the receiver. 'Hello.'

'Mrs Tebbit?'

'Yes. I'm Claire Tebbit.'

'This is Anne Johnson. I'm Steven's mother. He's a friend of James. James has just arrived here and he's very upset about a discovery he has just made. I think you should come round here and talk him through it. Do you have a car?'

'Of course.'

'It'll take you five minutes...'

Claire followed the directions and pulled up at the front gate. Anne Johnson was standing by the open front door. She held out her hand.

'I'm pleased to meet you... although this isn't a very auspicious moment.'

Claire followed her host into the living room where James sat on the sofa wiping his eyes, a box of Kleenex on his knee. A boy of his age sat beside him. On the table by the sofa were two documents. One was a small green, hard-covered booklet with a gold harp in the centre and three words in gold lettering in the top and bottom corners. By the booklet was a scruffy sheet of typewritten foolscap paper. Claire's heart began to thump and she broke out in a sweat. He knows, she thought. He's found Liam's passport and his death certificate. He knows that Dan is not his father and his surname is O'Malley not Braithwaite.

Chapter Eight

A few days later Daniel called from New York.

'I'll be home on Saturday morning.'

'Morning?'

'Yes. It's a night flight. Then I'll have four days off.'

'Oh, good,' said Claire with huge relief. 'I bet you need a break.' So do I, she thought.

'Yes. A break will be nice. How's James? Is he there?'

'No. He's just gone round to Steven's house,' lied Claire.

'How is he?'

'He's fine.'

'Looking forward to seeing his Dad?'

'Of course.' Claire realised, even more, that James's discovery that Daniel was not his father would be very painful for him.

'So James discovered all by himself that I'm not his father. That his father drowned fourteen years ago and we never told him.' Daniel could hardly believe what he was hearing. 'How did he find out?'

'He found Liam's Irish passport and his death certificate at the bottom of a kitchen drawer.'

'*In a kitchen drawer!* What were such important documents doing in a kitchen drawer? They should have been in a bank safe.'

'I forgot about them.'

Daniel sighed. 'You forgot you had put your husband's, James's father's passport and death certificate in a kitchen drawer.'

'Yes.'

'And when did James discover this... this rather vital fact about his life?'

'Last Wednesday.'

'And where were you when he found out?'

'Rehearsing for a concert.'

'Claire, James is left too much to his own devices. I've said so before... many times.'

'Yes, I know. What's the solution?'

'As I've said before: I think he should go to boarding school.'

'He won't like it.'

'He certainly doesn't like being left here on his own so much. Where is he now?'

'At Steven's house.'

'Since when?'

'Since last Wednesday – when he discovered the truth about his life.'

'The truth,' said Daniel bitterly. 'We should have told him the truth much sooner.'

At first James refused to return home.

'You're both liars,' he told Daniel when he called round to collect him from Steven's house a couple of hours later. 'You and Mum have lied to me for thirteen years. I've always believed that you were my real father but you're nothing but a sham. I don't want to live with you and Mum any more, but I can't live here either. It wouldn't be fair on Steven's family. They'd have to pay for my upkeep: my food and my clothes. It's not reasonable to expect another family to bring up someone else's son because he's been lied to by his parents.'

Daniel was in despair. He had never dealt with a young boy in such a tragic and difficult situation. It wasn't the time to mention boarding school. That prickly question would have to be faced later. It took Daniel over an hour to persuade James to return home. Steven's mother gave him a big farewell hug.

'You can visit us any time you wish, James. I'm sure you realise that.'

James climbed into the back seat of Daniel's car and they drove home in silence. On arriving home, James took the two precious documents out of his coat pocket, threw the coat on the floor and ran upstairs to his bedroom. He remained there for two days, refusing to come down for meals. Claire was utterly distraught. She had not expected James to react so violently to the discovery about his real father. Daniel was also upset and extremely anxious. After all, it was he who was largely responsible. He was the person who had posed as James's father for thirteen years. At the end of the second day, Claire and Daniel had their first serious discussion about the increasingly distressing situation.

'Should we call the doctor?' asked Daniel.

'What can he do?'

'Prescribe medication?'

'What for?'

'Anxiety. Being let down by his parents. Both his parents. We lied to him, Claire, and you know that full well. James lived his entire life trusting us – and we've both let him down extremely badly. I think we should book an appointment at the surgery. It certainly wouldn't be a mistake.'

The following morning Claire called the surgery and arranged an appointment for the three of them to see their GP. But James refused to go.

'What's the point? The doctor can't bring my real Dad back. It's a waste of time.'

So Claire and Daniel went to the surgery on their own and told the sad story to one of the GPs whom they had never met. When they had finished there was a deathly silence. It was the first time the doctor had heard such an extraordinary and harrowing story. He realised he had to give an opinion and offer advice, but as a young and rather inexperienced GP he wasn't sure how to handle such a delicate situation. He considered calling in a senior colleague, but quickly decided he should deal with it on his own. He crossed and re-crossed his legs, giving himself time to think.

'So you continued this camouflage in order to shield James, whose real father died young in such tragic circumstances.'

He deliberately avoided the word 'lie.' The couple in front of him had been doing their best to protect a thirteen year old boy.

'Yes,' replied Daniel. 'James thought I was his father. There was no question of there being anyone else.'

'And recently James discovered the vital documents in a kitchen drawer, proving that his father had died fourteen years ago.'

'Yes.'

'And of course the discovery upset him very badly.'

'Yes. It certainly has.'

'I'll call round to your house later and have a chat with James.'

'Thank you, doctor.' Claire and Daniel took this as a sign that the consultation was over and silently left the surgery.

The doctor called around later and chatted to James for a good twenty minutes, leaving a prescription for anti-depressants.

'Try going downstairs for dinner,' he suggested.

It took James over a month to recover from the shock of his discovery. He hardly spoke, ate very little and lost a great deal of weight. The shock also had its effect on Claire and Daniel. Claire cancelled her next chamber concert and Daniel took a week's holiday, rather over-due, from the LSO. Inevitably they began to drift apart. Neither completely blamed the other for the painful dilemma. Neither felt solely responsible themselves. It wasn't their own futures that were at stake. The future concerned James.

They all discussed the prospect of boarding school. Now James really wanted to board. The school they selected was partly weekly boarding and partly full boarding. James knew he would prefer to board full-time. It meant he would never be left on his own at weekends and he would make a completely new group of friends. Daniel agreed to pay the fees in full for which Claire was eternally grateful. Her chamber music performances were less regular and on the whole less well paid than Daniel's full-time position in the London Symphony Orchestra.

As expected, James did very well academically at his boarding school. He was in the top stream for most subjects and was usually near, or at the top of his class. Although he was less interested in sport, he managed to hold his own sufficiently well enough to secure a place in the Football Second Eleven. He avoided Rugby, which fortunately was no longer compulsory. There had been too many injuries over the years, some of them quite serious.

During James's first year at boarding school Claire and Daniel split up. As they had never married, there was no harrowing, time-consuming divorce. Once it had been established that Daniel was not James's father, they both realised they had little in common. Daniel visited James at home during the holidays and took him out to lunch at the weekends during term time. His relationship with Claire was now tenuous but supportable. He sorely missed being James's father and blamed himself for not telling James the truth much sooner.

The evening before James was due to return to school in the lower sixth form, Claire prepared his favourite dinner. She was exceedingly proud of her son, who had gained ten O Levels, eight with grade A and two with Grade B. She had opened a bottle of light white wine to celebrate the occasion. After all, James was now sixteen and a half years old. Time to discover alcohol – and how to deal with it. Halfway through dinner James posed the question that Claire had been expecting – and dreading – for over three years.

'Mum, are you in contact with anyone in Dad's family? I mean my real Dad, my birth father, not Daniel, an amazing substitute Dad though he is.'

As Claire refilled her wine glass her thoughts went back seventeen years. To Liam's court case where the rapist had got off with a caution 'for encouraging his victim.' Then the holiday on Achill Island in the shabby Achill Head Hotel, not far from Liam's birthplace in Westport, County Mayo. The evening when Liam had gone out fishing for mackerel with his childhood fishermen friends, followed by the storm that had blown up suddenly, capsizing the tiny boat and drowning all three of them. Then she remembered Liam's sister, Nora, cold and remote, who had virtually blamed her, Claire, for the storm that had drowned her brother; and the two week wait until the bodies were recovered. Then there was the Roman Catholic funeral into which she had had no input. 'As you're a foreigner you don't have to attend the wakes.' And finally, the funeral bill Nora had sent her, all itemised for almost three hundred pounds. Tears trickled down Claire's cheeks and quickly became heavy sobs. James shouldn't, mustn't know how shocking and tragic all the events had been. Now seventeen years ago, it seemed just like yesterday.

James came around the table and put his arms around his mother.

'Mum, I'm so sorry. I shouldn't have asked you. I didn't realise how upset you would be.'

Now James was even more determined than ever to visit the place of his father's birth, his life and death.

Claire was slowing beginning to understand that James needed to know more about Liam's family background – and his death. Until James was thirteen Daniel had been his father – his all. Daniel had also been an only child. Both his parents were killed in a plane crash when Daniel was only eight years old. A strict maiden aunt, who had been totally against Daniel becoming a professional musician, had brought him up. When he had won a scholarship to the Royal College of Music his aunt had virtually disowned him. Claire was finally beginning to understand that James was as important to Daniel as Daniel was to James. They remained closely in touch. They were now much closer than she was to Daniel and still needed each other.

Understandably, James now wanted to know more about his father's background: where he had been born; what the family house had been like; where he had gone to school; how, having been born in such a remote location, he had managed to win a scholarship to University College Dublin to study law. The questions were endless and as far as James was concerned, Claire had too few answers. She had very few photos of Liam. There were none of his childhood, just a graduation photo and their wedding photo, which Claire had now restored to its former and rightful place on her dressing table.

James was now eighteen and had finished his A Levels. As the custom was then in 1973, he was returning to school for a seventh term in the sixth form to try for a scholarship to King's College Cambridge. Like his father, James was planning to read law. At the end of his interview at King's, the professor told James that he had won a scholarship. The interview had been a gruelling experience lasting well over an hour and when the professor announced James's success, he smiled for the first time.

James was in seventh heaven. It was what he had been hoping, longing for, but finally hearing the good news was almost unbelievable. He rushed out to the quad in search of a public telephone. His first call was to Daniel, who had kept the afternoon free in the hope of good news. Daniel was ecstatic.

'That's wonderful news, James. Many congratulations. I'll call round tomorrow evening at seven and take you out for a celebratory dinner.'

Claire was equally delighted – and relieved that neither she nor Daniel would have to pick up the bill for the university fees.

'Well done, darling. What time will you be home? Shall I book *La Rotisserie* for eight o'clock?'

There were still many things to sort out. Would James be assigned digs on the university campus or would Claire have to find accommodation locally in the town? What about clothes? What were young men wearing at university in the 1970s? And what about money? James would need an allowance. He couldn't be expected to support himself. Claire realised she would have to discuss James's finances with Daniel, who had, after all, been James's official father for most of his life. Thank goodness for Daniel and his wonderful care.

James was over the moon. He couldn't imagine receiving a bigger prize - a scholarship to one of the world's most prestigious universities. And to add to the prize, he was about to follow in the footsteps of his father, a father whom he had never known, who had drowned nineteen years ago in one of the remotest locations in the British Isles. James felt the time had now come for him to visit Achill Island in County Mayo to try and pinpoint the exact spot where his father had drowned and maybe also visit his grave.

But first he had to find a temporary job. He realised he must finance the trip by himself. It wouldn't be fair to expect either his mother or Daniel to pay for his trip down Memory Lane, above all to such a remote location.

In the 1970s, many students waiting to go on to university either took a 'gap year' or a job. 'Gap years' usually included time abroad, either for paid employment or travel to remote places with a backpack. These were difficult to arrange, especially for students such as James, who had stayed on at school for a seventh term in the sixth form. So James sensibly dismissed the idea. It would undoubtedly involve expense, which would mean asking for Daniel's financial help. And Daniel had already been more than generous.

At that time jobs for young people without qualifications were limited, but they were available. And James did have four A Levels to his name, plus a scholarship to King's College Cambridge. The most common jobs for students were either serving in a shop, a pub or a restaurant. James thought through the options and decided that shop hours would be more civilised and more what he was used to. Also, it was November, so shops needed extra hands to help with the Christmas rush. James applied to Selfridges in Oxford Street and was offered a post in the toy department.

The toy department was massive, over-stocked and very hard work. However, James derived a certain satisfaction, even pleasure, from the work and stuck it out until mid-January. Then he secured a job at Simpson's, the well-known Gentlemen's Outfitter in Piccadilly. By mid-July he decided he had worked long enough on a shop floor and had, hopefully, earned enough for his fare to the West of Ireland.

Both Claire and Daniel were delighted at James's fortitude in working so long. Claire had arranged on-campus accommodation for James in early October. A financial grant had been arranged with the local council to fund his living expenses, which Daniel had promised to augment if necessary. Everything was set fair for James's student life in Cambridge.

Now all he needed to do before he went up to university was to visit the place of his father's birth, death and burial.

Chapter Nine

Donal O'Malley walked into the field where the sheep were grazing and closed the gate securely behind him. There were about thirty sheep of various ages, shapes and sizes and Donal knew he had to take at least five of them to the slaughter house. There wasn't enough grass for them to eat and he could no longer afford the fodder. That was the big problem in this Godforsaken spot in County Mayo – almost the most westerly point in Ireland. Only Achill Island and the tiny sea-bound islands beyond were further west. Leaning heavily on his stick, Donal limped on in the mizzling rain. Day and night it rained. Not heavy rain, just endless drizzle and the sun rarely shone. It wasn't only the lack of sun and endless rain that curbed any serious growth. It was more due to the fact that County Mayo was bog-bound. Less than three feet under the ground was solid, endless bog. Although perhaps solid wasn't the correct description, as the soggy soil constantly shifted, making the planting of any crops quite hopeless. Of course the bog could be dug out and turned into sods of turf, which would be burnt in fireplaces instead of coal. But the digging was hard labour; the turf sold for very little and at least three times the amount was needed to replace coal. There were many sites long abandoned and once digging had started, the ground was even more barren. Nothing grew and the uneven terrain was extremely treacherous for any animals reared there.

As Donal walked towards his flock, several of the sheep sidled up towards him. He fondled ears and patted backs. He knew them all and had names for most of them. It would be a difficult and painful process to decide which of them should go to the slaughterhouse. He made his sad decision, left the field and walked towards his cottage. There was a livestock market in Westport tomorrow. Maybe he could sell them rather than have them slaughtered. That would be less painful. As he approached the door of his run-down cottage, he stumbled over the latest shower of tiles that had slid down off the roof. Can't afford new tiles, he thought. Can't afford a roofer either. And I can't go up there on my own. Not with these legs.

He stood and stared at his shabby little cottage, despair rising up inside him. Why was he still living here, all alone, in such a pitiful state? Why hadn't he progressed, moved on to a better job, got married and gone to live in a more habitable property? But why had he become a farmer in the first place? Whose idea had it been? He remembered he had left school aged fourteen years old. At the time he was grateful. He wasn't in the least bit academic. Reading and writing had always been a great struggle. And as for arithmetic! It was all he could do to count up on his fingers, and like most people, he only had ten: a very limited number when it came to counting.

Was it his Dad's idea that he should become a farmer? Dolan didn't think his Dad had known much about farming. As far as he could remember, Dad had always been a clerk in Galway Town Court. Then there was his mother who had died so young, when he was only ten years old. Dolan always felt he had been worse off than his two brothers and two sisters, at the time aged between two and eight years old. He hadn't seen his older sister, Sinead for over ten years. She had accepted the first proposal of marriage with alacrity and had moved out of Westport to live in Dublin. Nora still lived in Westport, not because she wanted to, but because her husband, Seumas refused to live anywhere else. His brother, Dermot also lived in Dublin, having become, like their Dad, a clerk in Dublin's criminal court. Then there was the youngest and much the brightest sibling, Liam, who had drowned in a tragic fishing accident off Achill Island, just a few miles away at the age of only twenty-six. That was twenty years ago. Now he, Donal, was fifty-eight years old and twenty years ago seemed almost like yesterday.

Why hadn't he got married? He would have had someone to chat to, to share his meals and share his bed. But how could he have found anyone to marry him in this Godforsaken, abandoned part of the world? And who would have married him and been forced to put up with his filthy, slovenly habits? Sometimes he missed not having any children of his own. It would have been rewarding to watch them grow up and help them avoid life's many problems that he was facing every day, all on his own.

Dolan continued to stare at his dilapidated cottage, his despair mounting. But hunger was also mounting, so he realised he would have to find something to eat. He couldn't afford another pub lunch so soon after the last one only two days ago. He went inside to the kitchen and opened the fridge, a new acquisition strongly advised by Nora.

'Fridges are vital in today's modern world,' his sister had insisted. 'We've got two now – and a deep freeze.'

Donal couldn't imagine what Nora put in two fridges, never mind a freezer. What was wrong with meals in the pub? He was still poking around among the packages, searching for something to eat when the phone rang. More new modern equipment he thought, as he limped towards the phone and lifted up the heavy black handset. Shielding the mouthpiece with his other hand, he shouted down the receiver.

'Hello, there! Who is it?'

'It's Nora,' his sister's voice crackled along the line. 'How are you, Donal?'

'I'm fine thanks. And how's yerself?'

'Fine too, thanks, bro. I wondered if we could meet up for a chat.'

'A chat about what?'

'That'll evolve when we meet.'

'Evolve?'

'Come about.'

'Aah!'

'Tomorrow morning at eleven?'

'Fine.'

That'll postpone the decision about the sheep, thought Donal.

As arranged, Nora and Donal met in the pub. Looking around the scruffy, beer-stained walls and the scratched floor-boards, Nora's thoughts went back to the time twenty years ago, when Donal had driven her and their sister-in-law, Claire here for lunch. It was about a week after Liam's tragic accident and the pub had looked even worse then. Claire must have been in total shock, especially coming from such a cosmopolitan and sophisticated city as London. And she'd ordered a glass of white wine! Quite unheard of in County Mayo in those days. Colum had been quite perplexed and had gone to his house to fetch a bottle.

'I've had it some time,' he'd said. 'No one drinks wine around here.'

It was warm, but Claire had drunk it anyway. She had finished the bottle. But things had moved on in twenty years, even in rough remote pubs such as this one. Nora thought she would risk a glass herself. She could always send it back if it wasn't to her liking. Brian, Colum's son was very accommodating.

Nora passed James O'Malley's letter over to Dermot. 'This came the other day. I'd like you to read it.'

24 Arlington Avenue
Islington
London N1
Tel: CAN 0428
20 June 1974

Dear Aunt Nora,

As I'm sure you'll understand, this is not an easy letter to write. I believe that you and my mother, Claire O'Malley, lost contact after my father's tragic death in 1954. I never knew my father, as the accident happened nine months before I was born. I was brought up with the help of a friend of my mother's, Daniel Braithwaite, whose name I adopted. Until I was thirteen years old I didn't know that Daniel was not my real father. When I discovered the truth our lives changed completely. My mother could not cope with such a difficult situation and I was sent off to boarding school. I am now nineteen years of age and in October I will begin my law degree at King's College Cambridge.

I am informing you of all this because I have now reached the point in my life where I need to delve back into the past: my father's past. I would like to meet you and other members of the family and I would like to visit Achill Island and see for myself the place where my father drowned and also visit his grave. I am not asking for a bed in your house. That would be far too presumptuous. I plan to book a room at the Achill Head Hotel where my parents spent their last holiday together in 1954, before the tragic accident. I hope you will understand how much I want – and need – to understand my father's past life. I look forward to meeting you.

With warmest regards, James O'Malley.

Donal struggled slowly through the letter. Nora knew her brother found reading difficult and let him get on with it in his own time. She also knew there would be comments – and questions. She sipped her suitably chilled white wine and waited.

'I t'ink you should offer him a bed,' was Donal's first comment.

'But he wants to stay at the Achill Head,' objected Nora.

Donal gave a grunt. 'I don't t'ink he knows how bad it is.'

'As bad as twenty years ago?'

'I'd say so. Even t'ough t'ings have moved on out here in the last twenty years, I've still heard bad reports of t'e Achill Head.'

Donal picked up the letter again and studied it.

'Well, it's certainly news to me. Imagine being raised by someone who you t'ink is your Dad, but isn't. It must have been a terrible shock to the boy when he discovered t'at he wasn't his real Dad after all. So James, son of our brother Liam, wants to visit Achill Island and see where his father drowned all those years ago. D'you t'ink t'at's a good idea?'

'I don't know whether it's a good or a bad idea, but James is grown up now and must make his own decisions.'

'But don't let him go out in a boat.'

'I can't even stop that. But I'll write back to him and suggest that he stays a few days with us. Three or four should do.'

'Probably too long for him in t'is remote neck-of-the-woods.'

A week later James received the reply he was hoping for.

21 Briar Lane
Westport
Co Mayo
Republic of Ireland
Tel: 01 35 97524
30 June 1974

Dear James,

It was good to hear from you and I look forward to meeting you. I read your letter with great interest and understand why you want to revisit your late father's past.

I also appreciate why you would like to stay at the Achill Head Hotel. It was, after all, where your parents spent their last holiday together. But I'm not sure if you would find the hotel very comfortable – or welcoming. Most places in this remote part of Ireland have improved and moved on, but I gather this has not happened at the Achill Head Hotel. I would be more than happy to offer you a bed here for a few nights. You would probably find that long enough. I suggest that you book a flight to Shannon Airport via Aer Lingus and arrange a self-drive car. There is no public transport in the West of Ireland and you need to be able to get around independently.

Please give me a call on the above telephone number if you need any more help. I am looking forward to meeting you.

Warmest regards, Nora.

James put the letter down and thought hard. It was a welcoming letter and he was touched that Aunt Nora had offered him a bed for a few nights. But it seemed that transport in the West of Ireland was a problem. Or rather, there was no public transport at all, so anyone living there or visiting would have to supply their own. He would have to hire a car, but he hadn't yet learned to drive. Perhaps he could discuss the problem with Daniel? After all, Dan was still his replacement Dad. Since the great discovery, when James had found out that Daniel wasn't his father after all, the barriers of mistrust had slowly been repaired and James actually found Daniel a great deal easier to get on with than his mother. Dan was more relaxed and didn't worry. Claire worried incessantly about when the next chamber concert would take place and how much she would be paid.

There was no rush about learning to drive and James realised it would take him at least six months. It now looked as if he wouldn't be going to visit the West of Ireland until the following summer. He knew he would have to visit in the summer. From what he had heard of the weather in that remote part of the British Isles, it appeared that summer was the only possible time. And even the summer wasn't up to much. He would write a grateful letter to Aunt Nora explaining the situation and suggest he visit next year.

As James had hoped, and rather expected, Daniel was all in favour of the driving lessons.

'They're par for the course, James. Everyone must learn to drive, whatever they do, wherever they're travelling to. I'll foot the bill. Don't you worry about it.'

'Thanks a million, Dan.'

James tucked into his steak and French fries with relish. It was good to know that Dan was almost always on his side. It was strange how alike the names Dan and Dad sounded.

'Are you sure you should visit your father's birth and death place on your own? It might be quite stressful. Perhaps I should come along with you?'

'You're a star, Dan. You really are. Let's discuss it nearer the time.'

'Good idea.'

Daniel signalled to the waiter to bring the dessert menu.

James received Nora's reply within a week.

Dear James,

How foolish of me. Of course I should have realised that aged nineteen you mightn't be able to drive. However, I'm sure lessons can be arranged. Nowadays driving is an essential skill, wherever you live. Let me know how you get on. We can easily rearrange your visit for next year.

Warmest regards, Nora.

James began his driving lessons at the beginning of September, transferring the course to Cambridge when he went up to King's College. In the middle of April, just after Easter, he passed first time. He was cock 'o the hoop and extremely relieved. Now all he needed was a car.

At the beginning of May he wrote again to Nora.

Room 147
North Cloister
King's College Cambridge
Tel: Cambs 07941
7 May 1975

Dear Aunt Nora,

I'm delighted to give you the good news that I have just passed my driving test first time. I'll be able to put in plenty of practice before I visit you, hopefully towards the beginning of July.

Regards, James.

Chapter Ten

On 7 July 1975 James flew to Shannon Airport on his first visit to the West of Ireland. He had planned the date carefully so he would be on Achill Island for the twenty-first anniversary of his father's death on 9 July 1954. Daniel drove him to Heathrow Airport.

'Are you sure you'll be OK, James? You've never met your Dad's family and you'll be driving on remote unknown roads all on your own. The West of Ireland sounds a bleak place, especially Achill Island. I wish you'd let me come with you.'

Daniel stopped the car outside the passengers' departure entrance. As they stepped out of the car, he and James exchanged a fond hug.

'Don't worry, Dan. I'll be fine. I'm only away for four days.'

'You'll call me when you arrive?'

'Of course. If I can't find a phone at Shannon Airport I'll call you from Aunt Nora's house.'

'I hope you get on well with her – and with the rest of the family.'

'So do I,' said James with some feeling. 'But it's a short trip, thank goodness.'

'Your Aunt Nora will probably want to know why your mother isn't going with you.'

'I'm sure she will. I'll have some explaining to do.'

James and Claire had barely discussed his visit to the West of Ireland. Claire's only comment was: 'I don't know why you want to visit such a remote, ungodly place, James. Especially as it was where your father was drowned and buried.'

What his mother couldn't seem to understand was, that was the precise reason for his visit.

'Got all your travel documents and maps?' asked Daniel, as he lifted James's small suitcase out of the boot of his car.

'I hope so. If not I'll let you know when I call,' replied James roguishly.

James placed his case on a luggage trolley and they exchanged another hug. As Daniel slipped into the driver's seat he waved to James's back. I'm so lucky to have him, he thought.

Once in the hired car, James spread his map out on the passenger seat. He and Daniel had selected it with great care at Stanfords, the map speciality shop in Long Acre. They had traced the route together several times and James had made a list of the main towns along the way. Going north to Ennis and on to Galway Town seemed quite straightforward. After Galway Town there was a choice. The more scenic route led through James Joyce country to Letterfrack, with Lough Corrib on the right. But the more direct route was through Headford, Ballinrobe and then on to Westport with Lough Corrib on the left. James decided that as he would probably be doing plenty of sightseeing during the next few days, the best choice would be to take the more direct route. It interested and rather amused him that all the road signs were in Gaelic as well as English, with Gaelic at the top.

He had done some research into Irish history and was aware of the language problems as well as the religious ones.

James drove into Westport about seven thirty in the evening. As it was midsummer and so far west, it was still broad daylight. He found the house without difficulty, small and rather run down in a narrow side street. Parking the car, he took his suitcase out of the boot and opened the gate. Walking through the overgrown front garden, he arrived at a shabby front door and rang the bell. After several minutes an overweight, grey-haired lady in her mid-fifties opened the door. She extended her hand.

'You must be James. I do hope you've had a good journey. The roads around here aren't that easy for strangers. We were expecting you earlier, so we've just finished our tea.'

'Oh, I *am* sorry. I'd no idea you ate so early.'

'That's no problem. I've kept back some food for you. Would you like to see your room and have a little wash and brush up or would you like your meal first?'

'It doesn't really matter. Whatever's easier for you, Aunt Nora.'

'Well, if you'd like to eat now I can clear up while you're unpacking.'

As Nora led the way to the kitchen she called out: 'Seumas! James has just arrived and is going to have his tea.'

James sat down at the table laid with an unappetising plate of cold food, as heavy footsteps approached and a stout, unkempt-looking man came into the kitchen. James laid down his knife and fork, stood up and extended his hand.

Seumas squeezed James's hand tightly. 'Hello, James and welcome to Westport. I'm Seumas, the Irish version of James. I'm Nora's husband. Please don't let me interrupt your tea.'

James sat down and struggled with his food. When he had finished, Nora took his plate, and holding it under the running kitchen tap, she wiped it over with her hand and placed it on a plate rack above the sink. That's the dishwasher, thought James.

'Shall I show you to your room now, James?'

'That would be great. And do you think I could call London, just to let them know I've arrived?'

'You want to telephone London? That'll be expensive.'

James was surprised. 'I'll pay. It's just to let my mother know that I'm safe.'

James followed Nora up a steep narrow staircase to the top of the house. Nora opened the door to a small but pleasant and simply furnished room with a double bed, bedside table and a large wardrobe.

'I do hope you'll be comfortable here, James. It's only for three nights. Your mother spent over two weeks here after the downing tragedy.'

As soon as she had said it, she regretted it.

'I'm sure I'll be fine. Goodnight, Aunt Nora.'

'To bed so soon?'

'It's been quite a long day...'

'Are you sure you won't join Seumas and me for cocoa and biscuits at nine thirty?'

James felt it would be impolite to refuse. He looked at his watch. 'In about an hour?'

As he unpacked his wash bag and a few clothes, he looked around the bedroom. So this is where Mum slept after the terrible accident. Then it must be the house where Dad was brought up. I need to find out more, he thought.

An hour later, back in the kitchen, James's stomach heaved at the sight of the cocoa and biscuits. 'May I just have a glass of water, please?'

'Have you a plan for tomorrow?' enquired Nora when they were finally seated at the table, Seumas at the head.

'Not really. The big day for me is Sunday. You may remember that my father was drowned on 9 July, exactly twenty-one years ago?'

'I do indeed. And a terrible tragedy it was too.'

'Tell me, Aunt Nora: is this the house where my father was brought up? You mentioned earlier that my mother spent over two weeks in the bedroom upstairs where I'm sleeping now. It would help to fill in the gaps.'

'Indeed, it is the house where the O'Malley family grew up. And your Dad too, of course. When my Dad died all the rest of the family had moved away from Westport to live in Dublin. So it seemed logical that Seumas and I should have the house. We paid for it, of course. Quite a sum, wasn't it Seumas?'

'It certainly was at the time. I don't know how much it would cost now – but that no longer matters, does it Nora?'

'No, and indeed it doesn't.' Nora made it sound as though the discussion about money was inappropriate.

'Now tomorrow I'd thought we'd have a pub lunch with my brother, Donal. He's a great one for pubs, is Donal. And you'll have the chance to meet your Dad's older brother, James.'

'Sounds good to me.' James felt he couldn't refuse.

'Well, that's settled then. I'll call Donal in the morning. Do you like a cooked breakfast, James? You look as if you could do with one. A bit of extra flesh wouldn't hurt you.'

'Cooked breakfast?' James wondered what that involved.

'It's the custom in most West of Ireland families. Bacon, eggs, sausages, black pudding. All that sort of thing. Seumas enjoys his cooked breakfast, don't you Seumas? I have it ready for him at eight o'clock sharp.'

James wondered if Claire had had to cope with a cooked breakfast all those years ago. All she ate now was a yoghurt.

'If you don't mind, I'd rather skip the cooked breakfast.'

'That's fine by me. Maybe a lie-in will do you good.'

'Yes, I think so. Well, I'll go up now.' James stood up. 'Thank you so much for your kindness.'

'Oh, that's a pleasure. Sleep well now.'

To his surprise James slept well and was up by nine thirty. He looked around in the bathroom, hoping there was a shower, but there was only a bath. Down in the kitchen Nora asked if he would like some breakfast.

'Just a cup of coffee and a piece of toast, please.'

'That'll be plenty at this late hour,' advised Nora. 'Donal will be here at midday for our pub dinner.'

James's light snack finished, Nora took his plate and mug off the table and the same hand-washing routine as the night before took place under a running tap.

'Let's go and have a chat in the parlour – or what you would probably call the lounge,' suggested Nora.

James followed Nora into a rather bleak room with a bow window overlooking the front garden. A ragged, stained net-curtain shielded the occupants from any curious passers-by. The room was sparsely furnished. A sofa with sinking seats stood along the wall opposite the fireplace. There were three differently coloured leather armchairs and a footstool. The walls were painted dark cream, completely bare of paintings or any other decorations. There were no books, newspapers or photographs. Nora indicated one of the armchairs to James and sat down on the sofa. Then the comments and the questioning began.

Nora gave James a long hard look. 'You're the spitting image of your Dad, my brother Liam: tall, slim, dark hair, brown eyes. Have you seen many photos of him?'

'Just my parents' wedding photo and Dad's passport photo.'

'How did that come about?'

'I found his passport and death certificate at the bottom of a kitchen drawer.'

'In a kitchen drawer? How come?'

'Claire, my mother, said she'd lost it. That was how I discovered that Liam, not Daniel, was my real father. I was thirteen years old.'

Nora was too shocked to comment.

'Have you ever visited Ireland before?'

'No.'

'Not even Dublin?'

'No. Why would I visit Dublin? My Dad was born here.'

Nora went on to explain that her older sister and younger brother now lived in Dublin. 'They couldn't stand life here. Especially Sinead. She couldn't wait to get out, so she married the first man who proposed to her.'

James couldn't think of any reply to that remark.

'My brother, Dermot is doing well in Dublin,' Nora continued. 'He's a court clerk, as our Dad was. But of course it was your Dad, Liam who achieved the most in the O'Malley family, with his scholarship to University College Dublin.'

Their children, now in their twenties, lived in Dublin, Nora explained. She'd like to live in Dublin too, but Seumas refused to leave Westport. Nora decided it wasn't the moment to mention the terrible drowning tragedy. If necessary that could be discussed when James had visited his father's accident site on Achill Island on Sunday. Nora wanted to know all about Claire: how her health was; had she remarried; did she have an interesting job to keep her occupied and keep the wolves at bay. As the questions poured out, James began to feel as if he were in a courtroom. I suppose this is how it is, he thought. This is what awaits me. Perhaps this is a trial run.

Shortly before midday Donal arrived. Nora had tried to explain to James that her older brother was a little bit simple but well meaning.

'He's spent all of his life since he was fourteen working on farms. He doesn't know about anything else except farms – and pubs.'

Nora let Donal in and introduced him to James.

'Hello, James, and how are you now? Are you the posh part of the family?'

'I don't know about that, Uncle Dolan.'

'No need to "uncle" me, young man. I ain't no one's uncle. I'm just plain Dolan. Let's go out for our pub dinner. I could eat a horse.'

The pub lunch was a great deal better than James had expected. He didn't go to pubs that often. Claire and

Daniel had always been 'restaurant people.' At uni he had started to visit pubs now and again – but Irish pubs were a world apart.

'Have you seen much of the countryside around here, James?' enquired Dolan.

'No. I haven't seen anything yet. But I'm off to Achill Island tomorrow to see where my father was drowned. It's my reason for visiting the West of Ireland.'

'Ah, sure I know t'at. But maybe you'd like a little drive around? T'ere's no knowing when yous'll be back in t'is part of the world.'

'Yes. Thank you, Dolan. That sounds like a good idea.'

'You're not planning to show James around your farm, are you, Dolan?' asked Nora in some alarm. 'It's not like an English farm. It might put him off Ireland altogether.'

'Ah, no. Sure I wouldn't be doing t'at at all. My farm's not much of a sight – not at t'e moment. I t'ought I'd drive him past Croagh Patrick Mountain, wot his Dad and Uncle Dermot climbed. T'en we could drive around Letterfrack and t'rough James Joyce country. T'ere won't be much of t'at over in England. We might even make Galway Town. T'at depends when you're planning tea, Nora.'

'Let's make tea at six o'clock. Take care now.' Nora gave a wave as she drove off.

'I won't take ye to Achill Island as yous are going t'ere tomorrow,' explained Donal, as they climbed into his shabby farm truck. 'But I'll show ye some of the more remote parts of t'e West of Ireland.'

As they drove along another narrow unsurfaced road, with the Atlantic shimmering in the pale sunshine, Donal tried to explain the reason behind the bleak views and the extreme poverty.

'Tis a sad story, as so many Irish stories are. T'e climate's poor. T'ere's too much mizzling rain and very little sunshine. You're lucky to see a little bit of sunshine today, James. In t'e West of Ireland all t'e soil is boggy, which makes it difficult to grow anyt'ing. You's can dig it up and burn it, o' course, but it's a lot of work to produce enough for a decent fire. T'en a long time ago, I t'ink in the twelfth century, a greedy King of the Brits invaded Ireland. T'e Brits controlled everyt'ing and t'e Irish people had no say at all about how t'ey should live. T'en years later t'ere was t'e terrible potato famine. Half t'e people died or went to live in America.'

'Is that why there are so many ruined cottages?' James looked at the endless abandoned heaps of stone. No wonder Liam had wanted to leave Ireland.

'I'd say so. When t'e people died or went to America, t'e cottages slowly fell down. T'ere was no one to rebuild t'em – or live in t'em.'

'Dolan, please would you tell me a bit about the name O'Malley. Is it a common name around here?'

'I suppose not as common as it were before t'e dreadful famine. I t'ink many O'Malleys escaped to America to save t'eir lives an' all. But I believe it's considered a local name from County Mayo. But it's not t'at usual any more.'

'I've never met any O'Malleys in London.'

Dolan gave a little chuckle. 'I'm sure an' you haven't.'

A barren mountain loomed on the left. Here there were no ruined cottages, just heaps of randomly sited stones. Seagulls circled around, calling out in lonely bleak cries.

'What's the mountain called?' enquired James.

'Sure t'at's Croagh Patrick, t'e holy mountain of Ireland.'

'Holy? Why's that?'

'You've heard of Saint Patrick, Ireland's patron saint?'

'Oh, yes.' James thought of the lesson at school on the patron saints of the British Isles. 'But I don't remember a great deal about him.'

'Aah, sure. I can understand t'at, as you wasn't born and bred in Ireland. It's said t'at Saint Patrick was t'e founder of Ireland and brought Christianity to t'e country. When he arrived in t'e West of Ireland he climbed Croagh Patrick bare-foot and fasted at t'e top for forty days and nights.'

'He must have been very hungry by the end,' said James with some feeling.

'I'm sure he was. But God helped him t'rough it.'

Leaving Croagh Patrick behind, the track narrowed and turned sharply inland. As they drove on into increasingly desolate countryside, James's heart sank further. He was relieved that his visit to this remote part of the world was a brief one and wondered whether he would return ever again to visit his father's birthplace.

Arriving back at Nora's house for tea at the appointed time, James thanked Donal for the sightseeing tour.

Sunday 9 July dawned bright and fair. My big day, thought James, as he luxuriated in a hot bath.

'Good morning, James,' Nora greeted him. 'I assume you'll be going to Mass on this most important day of your life.'

'*Mass!*' James repeated. 'But I'm not a Catholic.'

'But Liam, your father, was a Catholic. Were you not brought up as one too?'

'Well, my Dad didn't bring me up. I never met him, as you know. Neither Daniel nor my mother are religious, so I wasn't brought up as anything.'

Nora clucked disapprovingly but said nothing. 'What time are you planning to leave?'

'When I'm ready. Aunt Nora, I've been thinking more and more about visiting my father's grave. Is it here, in Westport? Perhaps you could give me some directions. Is it far from here? Could I walk?'

'No, it's not far from here at all. About ten minutes, depending on how fast you walk. You turn left out of here and go straight up the hill. Then you'll see the church on the right. But it's Sunday, James. There'll be a Mass on. As you've never been to Mass you might find it quite difficult to understand. The service is all in Latin.'

'Latin? I thought it would be in Gaelic.'

'No. Always in Latin.'

'I'll see how I feel when I get there. Aunt Nora... do you ever visit my father's grave?'

'Yes. I do. Every year on the anniversary of Liam's burial. That will be in just over two weeks' time.'

'Is the grave tidy – well-kept?'

'Oh, it's quite tidy an' all. The church keeps it tidy for all those unfortunate people buried there.'

'Should I bring some flowers to leave on the grave?'

'You'd be lucky if you find a shop open on Sundays. Everything's shut around here on Sundays. Except for the church, of course. Will you be having lunch here?' Nora deliberately avoided Donal's description of 'dinner' at lunchtime.

'Thank you kindly, Aunt Nora, but I thought I might have lunch at the Achill Head Hotel.'

'Well, good luck to you. You'll certainly enjoy your tea here this evening. Let's make it at six thirty.'

'That's fine. I'll be back in good time.'

'You've got all the necessary maps?'

'Yes. Thank you.'

James decided to visit his father's grave first, before driving to Achill Island to see where he had drowned. Leaving all his maps and travel instructions on the front passenger seat of the hired car, he walked slowly up the hill, deep in thought. Just as Aunt Nora had described, the church appeared on the right, the door wide open. James stepped inside and stood at the back. The sound of strange music, like medieval monks chanting, echoed eerily around. He stood, watching and listening, for a good five minutes. Then, realising he must visit his father's grave and leave sufficient time to visit Achill Island, hopefully before lunch, he walked slowly towards the graveyard at the back of the church. As he had expected, the graveyard was sad and bleak, but reasonably well kept. James walked around, reading the inscriptions on the gravestones. It was a good ten minutes before he spotted the inscription reading: *Liam James O'Malley: death from drowning in 1954, aged 26.* Overwhelmed with grief, James knelt down on the damp grass in front of his father's tombstone, threw his arms around it and wept his heart out. Still sobbing, he rolled over onto the grass beside the tomb and almost fell asleep.

Finally pulling himself together, he stood up, wiped away his tears and made his way towards the front of the church. Walking past the open door, he heard a subdued murmur of voices. The worshippers were slowly filing out, shaking hands with the parish priest at the door, easily recognisable in his religious regalia. Not wishing to become involved with people he didn't know – or ever would know – James retraced his steps down the hill to Nora's house, where his smart rental car stood outside. Approaching the house from an uphill position, James was now in a good position to inspect it. My God it was shabby! It looked almost about to fall down. Was it this bad when Dad had lived here all those years ago or had it just steadily declined with many years of neglect? James realised he would never know. He also realised it was no concern of his. And fortunately, he would, almost certainly, never return to this part of the world again. Once he had inspected the spot where Liam had drowned, James knew he would never need to return to such a remote and Godforsaken spot ever again.

As he had done two days ago on his drive from Shannon Airport, James laid the map of the West of Ireland beside him on the passenger seat. Straight north through Newport, then directly west along Clew Bay. It should take less than an hour, he thought, starting up the engine. It'll be a nice little sightseeing trip, visiting the beach where Dad used to swim as a boy. I don't know how I'll handle seeing the spot where he drowned, but I'll have to cope with that when I'm there. And at least I've been to Dad's grave, so hopefully the worst part is now over.

As James turned left out of Newport, he could see the Atlantic Ocean sparkling in the sunshine. What a shame the sun is out so rarely in this beautiful, if remote part of the world. If there were more sun, there would be more tourists and the inhabitants wouldn't be so miserably impoverished. He reached the causeway and drove cautiously along a very narrow road. I wonder how many people came here before the causeway was built? There can't have been many people living here. The road widened a little and a large lumpy building appeared on the right with a battered sign reading *Achill Head Hotel*. James drove off the road and parked. Perhaps it would be a good idea to book lunch? After all, it was Sunday. Along the south coast of England, all the hotels and restaurants would be booked up days in advance. He slipped out of the driver's seat and walked up to the entrance. Another sign, also battered and rather crooked read: *Closed on Sundays*. Well, that's that, thought James. Should I drive or walk down to the beach? He decided to walk along the narrow bumpy track, turned a corner and there was Keel Strand, stretching out for several miles. He walked across a flat, stony section, which had once been a car park. Lying on the ground was a metal pole with a chipped sign saying: CAR PA... Imagine all this space, he thought, the silky sand, shimmering blue sea and no one here at all.

James sat down on a smooth rock and removed his trainers and socks. Completely oblivious to the fact that this was what his parents had done all those years ago, he tied his trainers together by the laces and hung them around his neck. Walking slowly down towards the sea, he felt the fine silvery sand slipping through his toes. Once at the water's edge, he paddled along the shore, small lapping waves replacing the sand. He stopped and looked out to sea. In the distance there was nothing to be seen. Nothing at all. Not even a small boat. America's over there, he thought, three thousand miles away. Several days by boat, depending on the size of the boat. Shielding his eyes with his hand, he continued to gaze out to sea.

And that's where Dad drowned. The Dad I never met. How different my life would have been if it hadn't been for that storm. He looked up at the fluffy white clouds scudding overhead. Up there is heaven. That's where Dad is: my real Dad, whom I never knew and never will know unless I go to heaven too. I wonder what it's like in heaven? Do the dead meet up with their relatives and friends? There was, of course, only one way to find out: to die and go to heaven. But how to die? That was the big question. And it might all go wrong. Perhaps loved ones didn't meet up in heaven. It was an impossible question to solve unless he died. And at only twenty years old James felt he was too young to tackle such a serious question. He gave a deep sigh and walked back up the beach.

Returning to the Achill Head Hotel, he thought he might give a knock, just in case there was someone there. He waited a few moments but to no avail. The hotel was completely shut up. Lunch? After the drive, and despite the emotion of visiting his father's burial ground and place of death, he felt quite hungry. No point in showing up at Aunt Nora's house. She was not someone who could cope with the unexpected. So he decided he would explore Newport. Even a pub would be better than nothing. And he would give Daniel a call. James knew Daniel wasn't away as he was picking him up from Heathrow tomorrow afternoon. Then he began to wonder why his mother hadn't offered to accompany him. Dan had offered – and he wasn't even his real father.

Something must have died in Claire when Liam drowned.

After lunch James called Daniel.

'All went well, Dan. I'm looking forward to returning home tomorrow. See you at the airport. Bye now.'

Home, he thought. Where's home? Can I really go back and live with Mum when she's had no input to my visit here? Of course I've got my digs at uni, but the holidays are long, far too long. Could I move in with Dan? He's been my unofficial Dad for the whole of my life. For thirteen years I thought he was my real Dad, then I discovered the lie. Even so, Dan has been a star. What would he think? What would Mum say? Maybe it would be worth giving it a try.

He drove back to Westport and arrived at Aunt Nora's house well in time for tea.